· J · CLARKE ·

Al Capsella Takes a Vacation

HENRY HOLT AND COMPANY · NEW YORK

To Geraldine O'Reilly
and her New Hampshire umbrella

Henry Holt and Company, Inc.
Publishers since 1866
115 West 18th Street
New York, New York 10011

Henry Holt is a registered
trademark of Henry Holt and Company, Inc.

Published in Canada by Fitzhenry & Whiteside Ltd.,
91 Granton Drive, Richmond Hill, Ontario L4B 2N5.
Originally published by the University
of Queensland Press in 1992.

Library of Congress Cataloging-in-Publication Data
Clarke, Judith.
Al Capsella takes a vacation / J. Clarke.
p.   cm.
Summary: Sixteen-year-old Al and his best friend, Lou,
vacation without their parents in the wild, partying beach
town of Scutchthorpe with unexpected results.
[1. Vacations—Fiction.   2. Friendship—Fiction.
3. Australia—Fiction.   4. Humorous stories.]   I. Title.
PZ7.C55365An   1992
[Fic]—dc20   92-35783

ISBN 0-8050-2685-1

First American Edition—1993

Printed in the United States of America
on acid-free paper. ∞
1   3   5   7   9   10   8   6   4   2

Al Capsella Takes a Vacation

$\mathcal{E}$very year, round the end of October, there's that one special evening when you wander outside and suddenly realise it's still light at seven o'clock! The air is soft, even warm; there's a scent of flowers and grass and the distant whine of a single lawn mower, and somewhere up the street you can bet three or four kids and a dog will be out playing cricket in someone's driveway. A feeling of excitement and happiness rushes up from deep inside you; it's as if something wonderful is coming, something far more wonderful than just summer, and Christmas, and fine weather.

It's the same with that first really hot day at school—the first day all the windows are left wide open after lunch and not even Mrs. Slewt tells you to shut them. Cherry Clagg is roaming round the classroom showing everyone the sunburn on her arms, half the boys have their school shirts unbuttoned, and the other half are wearing T-shirts anyway. The headmaster, King Arthur, stands up at assembly the next morning and announces that "teachers have counted" one hundred and fifteen boys wearing T-shirts instead of regulation school uniform and that sort of sloppiness isn't good enough for a school like Lawson High.

When he says this, the whole school turns and stares at Mr. Tweedie, the senior maths teacher. Everyone knows he did the counting, not because he's a telltale or has a thing about school uniforms, but because he's the only teacher on the staff who'd be able to concentrate on something as boring as that and really find it interesting. Perhaps because he's so small and weedy, it's fantastically easy to imagine Mr. Tweedie as a little kid; you can just picture him sitting in the back of his parents' car on the long drive up to Sydney: he's got a tiny little notebook and a stubby pencil in his hands, and he's counting every single telegraph pole along the Hume Highway.

This October, King Arthur went on for a very long time about the fine impression school uniforms make upon the general public; he'd just begun on some weird bullshit about how a neat and complete uniform was the True Indicator of a Healthy Mind when a year-seven kid fainted from standing in the sun too long. The assembly broke up. You could always count on the year sevens; most of the time they were real little pests, but you could rely on them for a diversion when it was most needed.

That first summery afternoon flowed on; windows wide open, a smell of mown grass wafting in from the oval, mingling with the faint scent of suntan oil from the girls who'd been sunbathing at lunchtime, a sleepy buzz of conversation about Christmas presents and summer holidays. And then our English teacher, Mrs. Slewt, walked into the classroom.

It's a funny thing about certain kinds of teachers—and Mrs. Slewt was definitely one of that number—their responses to great things like the first true summer day are so abnormal you could almost say they're not the responses of a human being. What did Mrs. Slewt do when she came into the room and saw the sun streaming through the windows and smelled that marvellous scent of peppery grass and suntan oil? She didn't tell us to pack up our books and come on a nature walk along Damper Creek, like good old Mossy Crockett had when she'd come to take us for Australian history in second period. No, Mrs. Slewt had a totally unnatural response; the summery weather simply put her in mind of the vacation essay. Straightaway she turned to the blackboard and started chalking up the topic in that spiky upright handwriting that always reminded me a row of pins stuck through the heart of a wax doll. Mrs. Slewt made a big mistake with that topic.

Ever since we could remember, even way back in prep at Mimosa State, where you did a finger painting instead of a composition, every single summer the set vacation topic had been "What We Did over the Christmas Holidays." It's true that since we'd hit high school it had gone under more sophisticated titles like "Seascape" or "Summer Dreaming," but it always boiled down to the same thing in practice, especially the practice of most of the kids in our English class. This year Mrs. Slewt broke all the rules. When she turned round from the blackboard and we saw the title she'd written up, there was an astonished gasp and then a long, disbelieving silence. Mrs. Slewt had written: "Why Do Birds Fly South in Winter?"

"But Mrs. Slewt!" wailed Emma Chipper, "We've *had* that essay topic. It was in the final exam paper!"

"It was in the midyear, too," called Melissa Pole.

"That's so," agreed Mrs. Slewt with a very small smile. The smile was phony—one of the first things you learn at school is that when a teacher is going to start an argument, and win, they'll always begin by pretending to agree with you. And they'll smile. "If you cast your minds back," Mrs. Slewt went on, emphasising the word *minds* in a way that suggested we hadn't any, "you may recall the question was also in last year's exams, both final and midyear." Her voice sharpened suddenly. "Why do you think that is, Andrew Macleod?"

She'd asked Macca because she could see he had one of his running shoes in his lap; he was inking in a neat checkerboard pattern with blue fluorescent marker.

Macca glanced up and smiled at her pleasantly. "I don't know, Mrs. Slewt." It was what you might call a generic answer, I suppose, undistinguished and suitable for any occasion. Macca used it a lot, like a stranger in a foreign land who has only mastered the first sentence in the local phrase book.

Mrs. Slewt tightened her narrow lips. "Andrew," she said, "has it ever occurred to you that one day you might deeply regret your lack of attention in class?"

Astonishment caused Macca to abandon his generic answer in favour of something more forceful. "Geez no, Mrs. Slewt."

Mrs. Slewt flushed. "I hope, for your sake, that may be so," she said coldly. "Now put that shoe back on your foot and listen!" She turned to the rest of us. "The topic appears so frequently," she explained, "for the simple reason that it's a popular question in the year-twelve external exam paper, which, in case it's slipped your minds, you'll be sitting for in less than twelve months' time."

At that moment I swear there wasn't a single person in the class who didn't feel Mrs. Slewt had lost all claim to be a member of the human race. To mention finals on such a day, when the sun shone and the holidays were just about visible and we still had them between us and our last year, was practically a criminal act. It was like telling a condemned prisoner who'd been given a last day outside that he'd better enjoy himself because he was going to be hanged the day after tomorrow.

Totally unaware of her insensitivity, Mrs. Slewt went on with her badgering. "The reason I'm setting it for the vacation topic is that though it's appeared in your exam papers for the last two years, no one, not One Single Person, has ever attempted it." She flicked an accusing glance towards Irma Doone, the school poet, who was good at English, but Irma was gazing dreamily through the window. "Not One Single Person," Mrs. Slewt repeated, her voice trembling slightly. She sounded like a kid who'd been promised a tricycle for so long she'd become afraid she'd be too big to ride it when Santa finally dropped it down the chimney. "So everyone, take out your calendars and make a note of the topic, *please!*"

"Mrs. Slewt!" Cherry Clagg jumped to her feet and Mrs. Slewt drew in her breath sharply. Cherry Clagg was so deeply numb in the normal academic sense that she was almost a kind of genius. It often took considerable brainwork on the teacher's part to answer her questions, or even figure out what they were about.

"Yes, Cherry?"

"Mrs. Slewt, I don't think it's fair that all of us have to write about birds' habits. The people who do biography learn stuff like that, they learn about animals and birds and things, but the ones who don't do biography don't." Cherry gave a large, gusty sigh and spread her arms out wide. "It just isn't fair!" She sat down again, arranging the pleats of her school skirt neatly over her big solid knees.

"Biography?" Mrs. Slewt had been teaching Cherry for five whole years, but she still hadn't got anywhere near the right wavelength.

"She means biology," Melissa explained in a bored voice.

"Oh." Mrs. Slewt tapped her pencil on the edge of her desk. "Cherry, let me explain something to you. Biology, or even ornithology, will be no real advantage to you in writing this essay."

"Ornithology?" whimpered Cherry. "What are orns?"

Mrs. Slewt pretended she hadn't heard. "And that applies to the rest of you," she went on. "We've been through this matter before, on several occasions, but I want to make sure you've all got it right. 'Why Do Birds Fly South in Winter?' is *not* intended to be an essay on birds. The title, as I've explained repeatedly, is a metaphor. Now, can anyone remember what a metaphor is?"

No one could. Oz Padkin, the school genius, was home with an allergy, Irma Doone was still rapt in the view outside the window, and my best friend Lou, the only other person who might have known, was hunched over his desk scribbling on a piece of paper.

The silence gathered. Joe Donaghue made a small nervous gesture with his hand and Mrs. Slewt glanced in his direction. "I don't want to hear anything about flags," she said repressively. Joe blushed. Last time she'd asked about metaphor he'd said it was a sign language with flags. Joe had once been a sea scout, but the real reason for his answer was that he had a problem: he got really edgy when no one answered a teacher's question; he couldn't stand the way the silence spun itself out, and he'd say just about anything to put an end to it.

"Well?" pressed Mrs. Slewt. No one said a word, and I saw Joe bite his lip hard to stop some crazy answer bursting out. I reckoned this time he'd say a metaphor was a second-year student at an American college.

I didn't have a clue what a metaphor was, even though Mrs. Slewt had explained it so many times. It was the kind of information that entered my mind like an ice pick, leaving a long, slim hole with nothing inside it. Whenever I saw the word in a book the only image it conveyed was a picture of Mrs. Slewt standing on a ship's deck, one arm extended stiffly, clutching a flag.

A few seconds more and Mrs. Slewt got sick of waiting and told us the answer herself; she did it better than us and it was quicker that way. She was just in time, too—Joe Donaghue's face had gone this funny shade of lilac and his hands were twitching all over his desk. "A metaphor," she informed us coldly, "is a figure of speech in which a name or descriptive term is transferred to some object to which it is not properly applicable."

Now the silence was like stone. "Can anyone give me an example?" she asked. Once again there were no takers. I glanced furtively round the class. Irma was still staring out of the window, Lou was scribbling busily, and everyone else had a distant, groggy expression on their faces.

"Louis Cadigorn," snapped Mrs. Slewt. "Are you doing your next period's homework in my class?"

Lou's head shot up. He covered the sheet of paper with his hand. "No, Mrs. Slewt."

"Would you mind telling me what you *are* doing? I gather you're not taking notes on metaphor."

"It's, I'm—I'm writing a letter, Mrs. Slewt."

"In that case, put it away at once, please. Answer your

mail in your own time." Her face went suddenly still and she blinked her eyes rapidly several times. We all knew what this meant: she was about to make a joke. And sure enough, out it came. "This isn't the *Correspondence School.*"

No one laughed. The kids who'd been looking elsewhere and missed those telltale blinks didn't even notice it was a joke. She needed one of those signs they had for television-show audiences, the kind that flashed red and said LAUGHTER. Or perhaps some kind of siren.

Lou folded his sheet of paper and crammed it into his shirt pocket, blushing furiously. There were whistles from the back row, but I didn't think for a moment that Lou would be writing a love letter. He was nervous with girls, and I couldn't imagine him writing to one in case she rang him up on the telephone and he'd have to speak to her.

"Can *anyone* give me an example of a metaphor?" Mrs. Slewt's voice had a real edge of desperation.

Joe Donaghue's nerve broke and he shot up his hand. Joe was a whiz at maths but hopeless at English, and everyone waited to hear what he'd say. "Uh—why do leaves fall down in autumn?" he ventured. You could see how he'd figured that one, I thought: sort of mathematically. If set X moving to place Y at season Z was a metaphor, then set A moving to place B at season C was another.

Mrs. Slewt wasn't mathematically inclined. "What is it a metaphor of?" she asked cruelly.

Joe looked confused. "Of?" he asked. "What do you mean, 'of'?"

"A metaphor must—" began Mrs. Slewt, but Emma Chipper interrupted.

" 'Why Do Birds Fly South in Winter?' could be a metaphor of 'What We Did over the Christmas Holidays,' couldn't it, Mrs. Slewt?" she asked brightly.

Mrs. Slewt slammed her book down on the desk. "Now listen to me," she said harshly. "I've already told you that I don't want essays on the travelling habits of birds. But there's something I want even less, and that's an essay on what you did over the Christmas Holidays."

"But, Mrs. Slewt—"

"In *any* shape or form, do you all understand?"

"Even if we use it as a metaphor?" asked Emma.

"Even then."

Irma Doone turned her face slowly from the window. "Mrs. Slewt," she murmured dreamily. "I've been thinking."

Mrs. Slewt looked up hopefully. "Yes, Irma?"

"I think you might be breaking a tradition here."

"A tradition, Irma?"

Irma frowned slightly, as if she didn't think Mrs. Slewt was taking the matter seriously enough. "Yes," she said. "For years and years, ever since kindergarten, every single summer we've been writing an essay on what we did over the Christmas holidays. And if this year we don't, if we write 'Why Do Birds Fly South in Winter?' it would be like leaving part of our lives behind, like—like finishing something forever."

There were tears in Irma's eyes, and several girls began reaching into pockets for their Kleenexes. Macca gave a long, piercing sniff, but it might have been his hay fever.

"Why," continued Irma, her voice breaking a little, "it would almost be like a—a death in the family."

"Oooh, Irma!" Cherry Clagg gasped, her round blue eyes growing large with horror.

Mrs. Slewt frowned thoughtfully. "Is there anyone else who feels like Irma?" she asked.

A forest of hands shot up. Most of the time, mentally at least, Irma Doone seemed to inhabit a different world from the rest of us. Perhaps she was miles above us, or miles below, perhaps it was just her creativity; the fact remained that when Irma expressed an idea in class, it was likely to be something no one else had even thought about. But there were sudden, rare occasions when she'd surprise us all by saying something right on target, something we all felt.

This was one of them; she'd struck a class nerve, we all wanted to keep on writing "What We Did over the Christmas Holidays" till the very end of our educational lives. Getting older seemed like a long process of leaving things behind, and though they were often things you didn't need anymore there was still a pang, as if a voice somewhere deep down inside you said: "Gone forever."

Mrs. Slewt counted the raised hands and got twenty-five, a full house. "In that case," she sighed, "as you all feel so strongly—" We held our breaths, waiting for her to give in. We should have known better: the small, sly smile appeared on her lips, and she went on, "And as I myself am quite determined that the vacation essay will be 'Why Do Birds Fly South in Winter?' I suggest you write your 'traditional' essay in your own time. I'll be happy to read them over, of course, though there won't be any credits given." She blinked her eyes rapidly. "A labour of love, you might say."

A long, long sigh wavered round the classroom and drifted through the open windows into the summery air outside. People began reaching into their bags and desks for notebooks and calendars; there was a faint scratching of pens as we took down the title of Mrs. Slewt's essay. Only Irma Doone remained aloof, her hands clasped under her chin, her large, protruding eyes staring mistily into space. But then, Irma didn't have a calendar; she didn't believe in dates and time and all that sort of stuff.

Cherry Clagg had something more to say. "Mrs. Slewt," she asked. "Can I write about my budgie? He doesn't fly south because he has to stay in his cage, but he's still a bird. He might *dream* about flying south."

Mrs. Slewt didn't reply.

2

$\mathcal{H}$ullo, boys." The voice was familiar but somehow totally unexpected, like hearing a bird chirp when you were
swimming deep underwater.

Lou and I were passing Safeway on our way home from
a cricket match, and the voice came from a plump lady
pushing a loaded trolley out through the sliding doors. A
tall, thin man walked beside her; he had the look of a museum attendant who'd just spotted a couple of four-year-
olds wiping their sticky fingers on the corner of some
priceless tapestry. I glanced at the stout lady; at that moment I could have sworn I'd never seen her before in my
life, yet she was obviously addressing us. Lou was no help;
he seemed shocked. His gaze swerved abruptly from the
lady's face down to the trolley, where frozen cakes were
sliding out of their plastic bags, a tumble of Sara Lees and
County Fayres and even the odd Plain Label. No wonder
the lady was plump, I thought.

"Hullo," I mumbled, still struggling to recognise the
face. The tall, thin guy looked me over silently, the way
people do when they've heard all about but never met
you. He wasn't smiling. The lady was watching Lou counting her cakes. There was a spark of real aggravation in her
eyes and when I saw that I suddenly began recognising all
kinds of familiar things about her: the frizzy hairstyle, the

small pointed nose, the way her two top teeth showed, faintly glistening, beneath her upper lip. It was Mrs. Slewt!

I can never recognise teachers out of school, walking around in an ordinary place. Perhaps it's because you get so used to seeing them standing with a blackboard behind their heads that the blackboard comes to seem like a part of them, and when it isn't there you feel disoriented; they're somehow hard to place.

Lou looked up from the trolley and caught the sharp glint in Mrs. Slewt's eye; it had a shocking effect on him. "Have a nice day," he chirped in a fake American accent, just like the checkout girls inside.

"You too," said Mrs. Slewt grimly, and she began to walk away with her trolley, the tall, thin man padding silently beside her. Halfway across the car park she whispered something to him and he turned round and give us another long, stony stare.

We walked on up the road rather more quickly than usual. "Geez, why did you have to say 'Have a nice day' like that?" I bleated. "She thought you were making fun of her."

Lou clutched at his wispy hair. "I don't know why I said it; I couldn't think of anything to say and then it just slipped out somehow—must have been that Safeway sign up behind her head." He swallowed. "They give you a real fright when they do that."

"Who? Do what?"

"Teachers. When they show up in the real world, like proper people. They shouldn't do it, it's—it's unsettling. What if she'd showed up on the cricket pitch just as I was getting ready to bat?"

I stared at him. "As if she'd do that! I mean, why would she?"

He stared back at me, still dazed. "I don't know. But seeing her there like that, slap-bang in front of a place like Safeway, gives you a creepy feeling. It's like an invasion—as if they're infiltrating the real world, like aliens."

"Oh, come off it. I'll admit she gave me a bit of a shock too, but she didn't come to Safeway just to frighten us. She was in there doing her shopping, and she happened to come out right as we were passing. After all, she's got to do shopping, she's got to eat. Hey, did you see all those cakes?"

He grinned at me. "Yeah!"

"And she's got to feed that thin guy as well; he looks like he could do with a good meal. Do you think he was her husband? I never figured she'd have a husband."

"Well, she is called *Mrs.* Slewt."

"Yeah, I know. But somehow you don't imagine them married—I mean, to real people. Real people who are actually *out* there."

"Now you're doing it," he said. "That guy didn't look like a real person to me, anyway. What do you think he does? Another teacher?"

"Some kind of museum attendant, the kind that keeps you out."

"Keeps you in, you mean. I reckon he's either a teacher or an admissions officer in the state asylum; he looked at us like he wanted to put us away." He lowered his voice. "Seeing teachers in the street makes you think it's the last days or something."

"The last days? The end of school, you mean?"

"The end of the *world*. You know, that bit in the Bible about monsters appearing on the face of the earth."

"Oh." His mood was all wrong for the season, I thought; even the sight of Mrs. Slewt and her grim companion couldn't quite spoil the perfect summer evening: sprinklers playing in the gardens and big fat magpies strolling beneath them, ruffling the drops of cool water from their wings and tails.

"Summer's really here," I murmured.

"So?"

"Well—holidays!"

Lou plodded on beside me without saying a word. Perhaps he hadn't heard. "Holidays," I repeated. "Only four weeks more to go!"

"Holidays!" he snorted. "Holidays!" He flopped down suddenly on the newly mown grass of the Bispins' nature strip. "Have you thought about that?" he asked. "Really thought?"

I sat down beside him. "Sure. I haven't been thinking of much else for the past few weeks."

"That's not thinking, that's *feeling*."

"What do you mean?"

He leaned closer to me, widening his eyes. "Have you ever considered, closely, what a holiday really *is*?"

"Sure—summer, no school, no homework. Well, hardly any," I added, uncomfortably recalling the vacation essay. "Beaches, cricket on television, feeling great all the time—"

"No." Lou shook his head. "That's kid stuff. Think about it. Really *think*—"

"Uh. Christmas presents, takeaway food, sleeping in every morning—"

"Nope. *I'll* tell you what holidays are really like. They're like . . . remember that time we walked into your kitchen and there was this big beautiful chocolate cake sitting on the bench and you said to your mother, 'Is that a real cake or is it one of yours?' "

You could hardly forget an incident like that. My mother, Mrs. Capsella, had acted like something let out of a high-security setup for a half-day excursion.

"Holidays are like that cake," said Lou. "They seem great from a distance, they seem real. But remember what that cake tasted like? Yuck! Holidays aren't real, they're *ours.*"

"Ours?"

"Yes, *ours*. They're *family* holidays. Get it? And for me, that means Bilbar." He clasped his head in his hands. "Four solid weeks at Bilbar."

"Oh." The Cadigorns had this holiday house called Bilbar out on the Peninsula. It was a nice place, right on the beach, but it was rather a small house, more of a shack, really. There was one biggish room and another small one that Mr. and Mrs. Cadigorn used as their bedroom. Lou slept on the couch in the main room, and guests slept on the floor. I'd gone there on a day visit a couple of holidays ago; Lou and I had spent most of our time outside on the beach, even though it was raining, and his parents had stayed inside. It was funny—when we'd gone out to the beach, Mr. Cadigorn had been fixing a window some hunters had broken over the winter and Mrs. Cadigorn had been washing a lettuce at the tiny sink. When we'd come back, some five hours later, Mr. Cadigorn had finished the window and was sitting on the couch, staring glumly into space, but Mrs. Cadigorn was still standing at the sink washing lettuce. It had worried me, somehow. I kept wondering about the lettuce—was it the same one she'd been washing when we left the shack? I told myself it couldn't be, that the Cadigorns had probably eaten the first one while we'd been out, but Mrs. Cadigorn's face made me feel uneasy. It was definitely the face of a woman who might have been washing the same lettuce for five hours.

"You've got nowhere to go in that place where you can be private," grumbled Lou. "If you want to write a letter or something."

"Write a letter?"

He flushed uncomfortably. "That was just an example. I meant if you wanted to do *anything* private, there's no way you can do it there without one of them barging in on you."

"It's a bit like that all the time. I mean, at home."

"But at least you can hear them coming; you get a few seconds' notice at least. There's only those two rooms at Bilbar, and that rotten outdoor bathroom thing. Even when they go to bed you can't be private; they keep on coming out of their room because it's so hot in there. And they hate me having friends to stay because then they can't come out and wander without having to get dressed." He moaned softly. "It's just *awful* there. I don't think I can face it this time."

He tugged at the neck of his T-shirt as if it was choking him. "And it's not just the privacy thing, either—there's nowhere to *go*, except to the beach, and you don't ever seem to meet anyone on that beach, not the sort of people you'd like to meet. It's a bay beach, there's no waves, it's the kind dads and mums take their little kiddies to, because it's *safe*." He pulled a face. "I think that's why they bought the dump in the first place, because I was a little kiddie then and they didn't want me to get drowned."

"What about Rosebud?" I asked. "It's only thirty miles from Bilbar; something must be going on there."

"Oh sure, there's all kinds of things happening at Rosebud, but it's too far to walk."

"Won't they drive you?"

"Nope. Not at night, when the things are going on. They say it's too far and they'd have to come back to the disco to pick me up. They won't let me hitch back, of course. And they say by the time they'd dropped me and got back to the shack it would be time for them to start driving back to Rosebud again."

It was all starting to sound uncomfortably familiar. I'd had some pretty frustrating holidays with my own parents, but at least we didn't have a holiday shack; we didn't have to keep going back to the very same place every single summer. There was a bit of variety in our boredom and frustration.

"The trouble is," Lou went on, "Mum and Dad don't really like the place themselves. Dad won't let Mum smoke in the shack because it's so tiny, and she can't smoke outside because there's fire warnings and litter signs all over the beach and the bush, so if she wants a cigarette she has to drive into town, and sit on the bench at the bus stop. As for Dad—once he's fixed up all the stuff the hunters broke in winter, he gets bored; you know he's always got to be doing something."

"So why don't they sell the place?"

"Because that would be admitting they'd made a mistake buying the joint at all."

"Sounds bad," I murmured.

"Oh, it is!"

Behind us, in the Bispins' front garden, I could hear the *snip snip snip* of Mrs. Bispin's pruning shears. I turned and saw her green sun visor bobbing among the bushes.

"He's got this mania—" Lou wailed suddenly.

"Who?"

"Dad. He's got this mania about Monopoly; he has to play it every single night. I think when he was a kid his folks wouldn't buy him a set. And he's always got to *win*. He gets really ratty if Mum or I get to buy Park Lane or Bond Street. And the table where we play has this wonky leg; it makes this noise: *wonka wonka wonka,* and when Mum or I throw a number that lands on something *he* wants, he always says it's because the table moved and he makes us throw again while he holds the leg firm."

"I didn't know your dad was like that."

"He's like that at *Bilbar*. The place does something to his personality; it brings out the worst in him. Once he had me playing there till four o'clock in the morning; he said if I told him I wanted to go to bed one more time he'd stop my pocket money for three whole months!" Lou drew in a long, shuddery breath. "That table goes *wonka wonka wonka* even if you breathe. When I'm sitting there, in that room, and I hear that noise, I get this— premonition."

"What kind of premonition?"

"Like when I'm forty-five I'll still be sitting there at Bilbar playing Monopoly with Mum and Dad."

"You wouldn't still be taking holidays with your folks when you're forty-five."

"But that's exactly how Bilbar makes me feel, like I still

might be." He gave a deep hollow groan and rolled over in the grass.

"Is anything wrong, boys?" Mrs. Bispin's green sun visor bobbed anxiously over the fence.

"Everything's fine, Mrs. Bispin," I assured her.

"Are you sure? Louis, are *you* all right?"

"Yes, Mrs. Bispin."

"I thought I heard you groaning, dear."

"I was just practising, Mrs. Bispin. For the—for the school Christmas pageant."

"He's going to be one of the oxen," I added, and when Mrs. Bispin smiled as though she might be going to ask if she could order some tickets, we got to our feet and moved off down the street. It was nearly dinnertime anyway.

When we reached Lou's gateway, he took one look down the drive and his face stiffened up.

"What's wrong?"

"Look!" he hissed.

Mr. Cadigorn was down in the garage, sawing away at something. "It's the wonka table," explained Lou. "He's trying to make the legs even. He's getting ready for the *holidays!*" He groaned again, the same low groan that had alarmed Mrs. Bispin. Startled, Mr. Cadigorn glanced up from his table, but when he saw it was only his son he went right back to his sawing.

"I just—can't face it!" sighed Lou.

An idea struck me. It seemed so simple, I wondered why I'd never had it before. "We could go somewhere by ourselves," I suggested. "You know, without *them.*"

"By ourselves? How? Where?"

How could be a bit of a problem, I thought. But I certainly knew *where*. I had no doubt of it. "Scutchthorpe," I said.

3

S
cutchthorpe!

It was Broadside Williams who'd discovered Scutchthorpe. Although Broadside had left our school almost a year ago, he'd lingered on in all our minds as a sort of hero, a kid who did all the things the rest of us dreamed of doing if we hadn't been hung over by parents and teachers and our own wimpish inhibitions. Broadside had holidayed at Scutchthorpe last summer; he'd gone with a mate of his. That in itself showed his superiority; there's no way Broadside would ever have considered going on holiday with his parents, even when he was ten years old. His choice of destination showed us up, too; we were just dreamers, we lay on our beds imagining ourselves in places like Bali or Honolulu or Las Vegas, tanned and taller, wearing romantic white suits like the guys in the liquor advertisements. Broadside didn't go in for daydreaming, he was a man of action. He just headed up the coast and found a real place that outclassed all our childish fantasies.

Scutchthorpe was a seaside town just a few hours' drive out of Melbourne. If none of us had ever heard of it before, and none of us had, our ignorance was just another mark of childishness. We didn't have friends with old utilities, like Broadside; if we'd gone up the coast it would have been in the backs of our parents' cars, and they wouldn't have stopped at a place like Scutchthorpe. Broadside told us he hadn't seen a single person over twenty-four the whole two weeks he'd been there.

Perhaps the noise level helped to keep them away, because although the town was small there were five discos in the main street and a few more in the back ones, and they were the sort of joints that never asked for ID even if you were four foot six with braces on your teeth. The lights never went out at Scutchthorpe, Broadside said. Main Street was bright as day at four o'clock in the morning and the nearest cop-shop was seventy kilometres away. The sun always shone, the kind of sun where you got an even tan, never burned or came out in blotches, and the surf was always up. There were no little kiddies on the beach because it wasn't a safe place for the kindergarten set. You could make out with a girl all day long on the sand and not once would you look up to find a toddler about to tip the contents of his plastic bucket over your head. There were no flags you had to keep between, and no brawny lifeguard with the kind of psychological problem that made him clamber down from his lookout when he saw a kid with a surfboard, just so he could direct him down to the rocky area reserved for canines.

Scutchthorpe! Whenever I thought of the place, this line of poetry would come into my head: *"With shawms, and with cymbals, and harps of gold."* I don't know where I got it from because I never read poetry. There was something about the tone of Mrs. Slewt's voice when she read the stuff aloud to us that put you right off it, possibly for life. I suspected the line had actually come to me from Irma Doone. She had a habit of standing up suddenly in class—any class: maths, biology, consumer studies—and reciting several lines of poetry; then she'd sit right down again. Broadside Williams hadn't said anything about shawms, of course, or even harps and cymbals; poetry wasn't his style either. I suppose it was just that Scutchthorpe sounded like the most perfect freedom, and freedom was heavenly music to all of us.

Why shouldn't Lou and I go to Scutchthorpe? It wasn't far away; in terms of distance it was well within reach. And we had enough money for a holiday of our own; it said a lot about the restrictions on our social life that we still had money saved from our last holiday jobs. No, the problem was the one it always seemed to be with anything you really wanted to do in life! Parents. Watchdogs.

■ ■ ■

"You ask yours first," urged Lou, when we'd let a week slip by without mentioning the matter at home, and the holidays were getting nearer and nearer. Only three weeks to go, and if we didn't act soon Scutchthorpe was sure to be all booked out.

"Why me?"

"I just can't risk it at the moment. Dad's in a really bad mood. You know how he was fixing the wonka table?"

I nodded.

"He can't seem to get the legs even. He's been sawing bits off every night this week and no matter what he does it still wonks. So then he saws a bit more off. The whole thing is getting shorter and shorter; if he goes on much longer we'll have to sit on the floor to play, because the chairs will be too tall. They're plastic, so he won't be able to shorten them. He's going to have to buy a new table and you know how stingy he is." He looked at me pleadingly. "If you ask yours first and they say yes then mine are more likely to say yes as well; they'll feel threatened. You know what they're like, real sheep. They're always wanking on about *us* being victims of peer pressure, but they're even worse."

"Okay," I said glumly. If we waited till Mr. Cadigorn got into a good mood we'd be qualified for the old-age pension before we even got a glimpse of Scutchthorpe.

■ ■ ■

"Mum, have you thought about where we're going on holidays yet?"

Mrs. Capsella was sitting at the desk in her study, staring gloomily at a blank piece of paper. She's a writer by trade, and part of the reason I can never take Mrs. Slewt seriously is that she believes writers write; that they are dedicated, busy people who cover reams of paper every day. Mrs. Capsella scribbled occasionally, but mostly she stared. She stared at pieces of paper, or typewriter keys, she stared at the walls and outside the window, and sometimes she just stared at nothing at all.

"What?" Mrs. Capsella looked up blearily. It always shocked her slightly when you disturbed the staring process.

"Have you arranged anything about our holidays yet?"

"Uh, I haven't got round to thinking about it, Al," she replied. Her tone was vague and shifty and I knew this was because she didn't like holidays much. She liked lying on the beach all right, or standing ankle deep in the water staring out at the horizon, but she didn't care for the cooking and shopping our holidays always seemed to involve. At home she could weasel out of stuff like that by saying she'd been working all day; she didn't have those kind of excuses when we were holed up in a holiday shack. She could have solved the problem by booking us into a place where meals were provided, but she had this two-part fantasy about holidays.

The first part was that holidays had to be "away from it all"—in places that were at least fifty miles from a town, even a very small sort of town, and ten miles from the nearest convenience store. As the crow flies. We weren't crows, but I certainly felt like one after two weeks spent in places like that.

The second part of the fantasy was that you had to be near the sea, and this provided a curious drawback in the shape of my father, Mr. Capsella, who had a thing about sand. He hated it; he hated to sit on a beach because the sand blew in his eyes while he was reading and made the pages of his books all gritty to the touch. He didn't even like to walk on the sand; he said it was too hot for the skin of his feet and he always kept his shoes and socks on to prevent blisters. If the *wonka wonka wonka* of Mr. Cadigorn's Monopoly table was the soundtrack for Lou's holiday nightmares, mine was the *flump flump flump* of Mr. Capsella's laceups ploughing through a row of sandhills. I couldn't take a swim without feeling guilty; I'd look back over the cool waves and see the pair of them huddled back on the beach, Mr. Capsella flicking specks of sand from the pages of his book and Mrs. Capsella brooding over what she was going to cook for dinner.

"I'll think about holidays next week," she told me. "I'm a bit busy just now." As if to prove it, she picked up her pen, lowered her head, and wrote "Chapter 1" on the top of the blank sheet of paper.

"Look, Mum, don't worry about it. The reason I asked you is that, er, the thing is—"

She lifted her head. "The thing is what?"

"It's Lou. He doesn't want to go to Bilbar anymore."

"Does he want to come with us?" She put down her pen and turned to me with an air of true martyrdom. "I suppose if I'm going to be cooking meals for three people, I may as well cook for four."

"He doesn't want to come with us, not exactly. Not with *us*, just with me."

She looked at me blankly. "What do you mean?"

"Mum, you know we're both sixteen now, don't you?"

"Of course."

"And we've both got quite a bit of money saved up, so we were thinking . . . we were thinking we might go off somewhere together, just the two of us."

"You mean you're moving out?" Her voice rose in panic. "You can't do that! You haven't finished school yet, you—"

"Calm down, Mum. We're not moving out. We're just going on a holiday together. There's this place called Scutchthorpe, where—" I hesitated. Even the name of Broadside Williams could have a negative effect on parents. "Where a friend of ours went last summer."

"Scutchthorpe?"

"It's this little town up the coast, Mum, just a couple of hundred miles away. It's a really *safe* sort of place; this friend of ours was there two whole weeks and not a single thing happened to him." Not the kind of things she worried about, anyway, I thought.

Mrs. Capsella was silent. She was gathering her resources, I knew; amassing misinformation of the kind she specialised in: horror stories from the newspapers she'd got all out of proportion, statistics on drugs, murders, and missing children that were way out of line—if she'd had them right, there wouldn't be a soul under eighteen left living in Australia.

I decided to apply a little moral pressure. Mrs. Capsella has a slight guilt complex about being overprotective, especially when I point out my age to her. The trouble is that she only suffers from the complex sometimes, when nothing important is in question. As soon as anything that matters comes up, she forgets all about being guilty.

"It's good for kids' development to go away on their own," I said. "They can learn a lot about, uh, making responsible decisions and, um, organising their time." I was using the vocabulary that frequently appeared on my school reports, generally in a negative context, and I saw her eyelids flicker. She was weighing up the dangers of death by misadventure against the possibility of educational advantages.

"Yes, but there are so many accidents at holiday time," she sighed.

"Statistically, Mum, in last year's finals class, not one single person got drowned in the summer vacation, but seventeen failed English."

She stared at the wall.

"And it would be great for Lou," I urged. "He's been really nervous lately. All that stress."

"What stress?"

"You know, just the usual kind: school, exams, home life, that sort of thing. Only Lou's a more nervous type than I am, than anyone is, really. And then Mr. Cadigorn gets awfully funny when they're at Bilbar."

Her eyes glinted. She loved hearing stories about other peoples' parents. "How does he go funny?"

"He turns into a tyrant. He makes them play Monopoly every night and no one's allowed to go to bed until he's cleaned up the board, even if it's seven o'clock in the morning. And Mrs. Cadigorn has to drive into the town if she wants to smoke; she sits on the bench at the bus stop and people stare at her."

Mrs. Capsella chewed on the end of her pen. "You know," she began, "it's been scientifically proved—"

Every time she used this phrase I had the odd feeling she was going to start talking about toothpaste brands. She didn't, of course.

"—scientifically proved," she went on, "that holidays are actually far more stressful for people than work. There are more marriage breakups, domestic murders, and suicides during the holidays than at any other time of year. Why, Dasher had this case just last February—"

Dasher, my mother's friend, was a psychologist. "What case?"

"This poor girl, about your age, who'd gone on holiday in one of those campervan things with her parents, her three little brothers, and the family dog. They couldn't get the van roof to go up properly—you know, there's supposed to be this space above the top bunks—and when it wouldn't go up, this poor girl had to sleep with the roof a few centimetres from her face. She'd been doing Edgar Allan Poe for year-ten English, and when she'd wake in the night—and she woke up a lot because there were wombats in the dustbins outside and the wombats made the dog bark and the dog woke the little brothers and they'd start yelling and throwing pillows around—"

The look of horror on my face stopped Mrs. Capsella in mid-flow. "What's the matter?"

"What's the *matter*? That girl didn't *go* on a holiday, Mum, she was *taken*."

"Of course she was. No one leaves their child at home when they go on holiday; it's a shocking thing to do. What on earth would the poor girl do, with the whole house to herself?"

I decided not to enlighten her.

"Anyway, as I was saying, whenever she woke up at night, she'd get the idea that the roof looked nearer than it had been, as if it was slowly closing in on her, like things close in on people in Edgar Allan Poe stories. And now the poor girl just can't—"

"Can't what?"

"Oh, I'd better not tell you any more. After all, Dasher's cases are confidential."

"Is she all right, though?" I asked anxiously.

"As right as she'll ever be, I suppose," Mrs. Capsella said gloomily.

"Listen, don't tell that story when Lou's around," I warned her. "He's too nervous for a story like that just now, especially if he has to go to Bilbar after all."

"Oh, Lou is just a very sensitive boy," said Mrs. Capsella fondly.

Sensitive. This is the word parents use when they're talking about someone else's kid. If I'd gone on like Lou did sometimes, she and Dasher would have had me lined up for a straitjacket in no time at all.

"Though I agree," she murmured, "that Bilbar doesn't sound quite right for him."

"Oh, it isn't!" I cried. "He needs to get away on his own for a bit. The thing that's worrying me, Mum, is Mrs. Cadigorn."

"Mrs. Cadigorn? You mean something might happen to her while she's sitting at that bus stop?"

"No, no, Mum. I'm sure the bus stop is a safe place to sit. What I meant is that Mrs. Cadigorn is a bit *overprotective*. She's always worried something might happen to Lou when he's out of her sight." I paused. "She acts like he's six instead of sixteen; it's bad for his development. It might even be why he's so nervous."

Mrs. Capsella fell right into the trap. "Barbara Cadigorn is a bit like that," she said happily. "And anxiety is communicable."

"I'm worried she won't let Lou go to Scutchthorpe because she's so anxious. And honestly, she hasn't got a thing to worry about; it's all in her mind. Like I told you, not a single thing happened to that friend of ours all the time he was there. He was safer than he would have been with his parents."

"Oh, I'm sure she'll let him go," said Mrs. Capsella breezily. "It's for his own good and theirs too, really. It's funny how difficult some parents can be about that sort of thing. I'll have a word with her if you like."

"Will you, Mum? Does that mean I can go?"

"What? Go where?"

"To Scutchthorpe. That's what we're talking about, isn't it? Lou and I going on a holiday together. And if you're going to talk Mrs. Cadigorn into letting him go, then it would look a bit odd if you weren't letting me, wouldn't it?"

There was an expression of dumb bewilderment on her face, like a not very smart dog when you throw him two balls at once, in different directions.

"Wouldn't it?" I pressed.

"I suppose—so."

"So that means we're going. Great! I'll just go and tell Lou."

"Hold on! Just a minute, I—"

"You mean you've changed your mind? But you *said*—"

"No, no, I didn't say, I didn't say—oh, of course you can go!" She gazed at me mournfully, as if already she saw the horror placard in front of the newsagents: TEENAGERS LOST AT SEA.

I felt a bit sorry for her.

4

*I*t was all set up.

It was hard to believe, but the Cadigorns hadn't made any trouble at all. Hard to believe unless you knew the peculiar circumstances, that is: the very same evening I'd spoken to Mrs. Capsella, Lou had come home to find his father in a surprisingly good mood, so good you could almost call it crazy. Mr. Cadigorn had finally succeeded in getting the legs of the wonka table even. The fact that it was only twenty centimetres from the ground had escaped his notice for the present. He was celebrating with a bottle of wine. "Sure," he agreed, when Lou seized his chance and asked about the holiday in Scutchthorpe. "You go ahead." And Mrs. Cadigorn had been in such a good mood to find Mr. Cadigorn in one that she'd forgotten all about being overprotective.

"They didn't give me a single, solitary argument," said Lou. "You'd think they would, wouldn't you? After all, I'm only just sixteen."

"What are you on about, 'only just sixteen'? We must be the only sixteen-year-olds left in the entire country who had to ask our parents' permission to take a holiday on our own! We're practically—what's that word for things left over from another age?"

"Anachronisms."

"That's it. We're anachronisms."

"But that's not what I mean. What I mean is—look, I'm sixteen now, right?"

"Right."

"And in a year or so"—he crossed his fingers—"I'll be finished school; I could be"—for some mysterious reason he blushed—"I could be anywhere! This might be one of their very last chances to have a real family holiday, all of us together at Bilbar, like we've always been."

You'd think I'd be surprised by that, wouldn't you? For weeks he'd been whingeing on about how much he hated Bilbar and how being cooped up in the place gave him a premonition that he'd still be spending his summer vacations there at forty-five. But give him a chance to escape and he wanted to be right back at the wonka table. I wasn't in the least surprised; Lou had been my best friend since the days of Mrs. Dirago's kindergarten and I'd got used to the way he felt and thought. He was the kind of person who, if he'd had a spare ear growing out of the back of his head, would have begun missing the thing the moment the doctors had cut it off.

So I didn't waste my time pointing out the obvious. Instead, I said casually, "I bet that table still goes *wonka wonka wonka*. That's why your dad opened the bottle of wine; then after he'd drunk a few glasses he'd start thinking he really had solved the problem, or else . . ." I tailed off deliberately, leaving a tantalising silence.

"Or else what?" asked Lou nervously.

"Or else, he'd say to himself, 'What the hell! I don't care if it shakes like a jelly and they keep landing on Park Lane. I'm a great guy, a born achiever, and I'll win the game whether the table shakes or not—and I'll bloody make sure *they* don't win if we have to play for forty-eight hours straight!'"

Lou had a very pale complexion, almost dead white, so that when he got nervous he didn't turn pale, because there wasn't any colour in his cheeks to vanish. Instead, the skin under his eyes would get a sudden shadow on it, faint and greyish green. I watched the shadow appear now. I felt slightly cruel, but as my grandmother Pearly Blount says when she's getting her own way at the expense of other people, sometimes you have to be cruel to be kind.

"Hmmm," muttered Lou, and I could tell he was thinking it over.

■ ■ ■

That week Mrs. Capsella booked us into Kooka Kabins, where Broadside and his mate had stayed at Scutchthorpe.

"It *was* Kooka Kabin, wasn't it?" Mrs. Capsella asked me. "Kooka Kabin, Scutchthorpe?"

"Kooka Kabins."

"Same thing. I just wanted to be absolutely sure I'd got it right; I wouldn't want to get you into the wrong place. And it *was* Scutchthorpe?"

"Yeah."

"Oh. How come you chose Scutchthorpe?"

"I told you. This friend of ours went there."

"And he liked it, did he?"

"He said it was great."

"Oh," she sighed, hovering uncertainly in the doorway. I had a pretty good idea what was going on in her mind. She was worrying about the holiday, she didn't want to look overprotective, so she was going to try and put me off. Any moment now she'd start telling me the guy at the Tourist Bureau had told her that Scutchthorpe had the lowest hours of sunshine for any coastal town in the country or that we had the only rooms in the town that weren't booked out for some religious conference.

"It's an awful name, isn't it?" she began.

"What?"

"Scutchthorpe. It reminds you of soggy toast crusts glugging down a sinkhole."

What could you say to that? Absolutely nothing. I edged past her through the doorway.

"Where are you going?"

"Just up to the Cadigorns' place," I said calmly. "We have to make a packing list."

■　■　■

"Have you thought about how we're going to get there?" I asked Lou.

"Don't count on *him*." He stared coldly through the back door. Across the lawn in the garage, Mr. Cadigorn was tinkering with the pieces of a diseased-looking table-lamp. I could tell from the cut of its jib, as my grandfather Neddy Blount would say, that the lamp was Bilbar equipment.

"*He* won't be driving us," muttered Lou. "Do you know why?" He spoke in a low, bitter tone. "They're actually going up to Bilbar two days early, now they've got shot of me. They're going to drive up the long way and stay the weekend in one of those fancy hotels. You know the sort of thing: 'Romantic olde worlde atmosphere, dinners by candlelight, champagne breakfast for two.'" He puffed out his pale cheeks. "In all the years and years we've been going to Bilbar they've never taken me to one of those places, not once. What do you think of that?"

"Uh, well, those kind of dumps don't cater for people bringing kids. They're too fancy. Bringing a kid would be like bringing an untrained Doberman; they'd just chuck you out."

"All the same—" His face grew fat with outrage as a fresh thought struck him. "They're leaving me alone here for two whole days without any food! Mum says she wants to clean the fridge out and I can eat takeaway. They might even turn off the electricity so I won't forget to do it."

Eat takeaway! It sounded great to me, and a few days back it would have sounded great to him as well. It was always better to point out the positive aspects of a situation to Lou when he was in this sort of mood. "At least you'll be able to write a letter in private," I remarked.

He rounded on me furiously. "Who says I want to write a letter?"

Avoiding one nerve, I'd unexpectedly struck another. I shrugged. "Well, you said—"

He changed the subject abruptly. "Looks like your father will be driving us."

Now *I* was nervous. The Capsellas' driving would have turned an ironman to jelly. Not that Mrs. Capsella got much chance to try her hand while Mr. Capsella was in the car; he put a high value on his own personal safety. But he was almost as bad himself; he had a passion for "shortcuts" and no sense of direction at all. If Queen Isabella had put Mr. Capsella on her payroll, Washington would have been the capital of Antarctica. Then, too, Mr. Capsella demanded complete silence when he drove; he insisted that driving required absolute concentration.

The enforced silence was a big strain on Mrs. Capsella, who liked to talk a lot when she was confined in a small, moving space. It was a big strain on me, too, having to keep quiet when I glimpsed a signpost that definitely suggested we were on the road back to town without ever having come near our destination. Though there weren't all that many signposts along Mr. Capsella's shortcuts; the Roads Department didn't bother to put them up in the kind of wastelands where he lost us. It could well take us a day and a half to get to Scutchthorpe, I figured, even though Broadside and his mate had made the journey in a couple of hours.

And there was something else. Broadside and his mate had arrived in their own vehicle. They hadn't been driven into Scutchthorpe by their parents, like a couple of eight-year-olds going to Cub Camp; they hadn't run the risk of being farewelled by their mother slap-bang in public. I shivered; that kind of thing could give you a bad start socially.

"If only we had our own car," I sighed.

"Yeah," agreed Lou. "Though it wouldn't be much use when neither of us can drive." His face brightened suddenly. "Hey! Skull Murphy's got his licence. We could go with him. I mean, he could go with us. I was talking to him the other day and he doesn't want to go to Tassie with his parents; he's got five little brothers and sisters."

"But Skull hasn't got a car, remember? He stacked it."

Lou's face fell. "Oh, yeah."

We sat there in silence for a few minutes, thinking.

Then Lou said, "Perhaps we could borrow a car from someone, and Skull could drive it."

"Like who?"

"Like—" He glanced at me with a meaning expression in his eyes. I didn't catch on at first. "Someone's folks."

"Not Skull's, not after that stack. His dad won't even let him sit in the front."

"Not *Skull's* folks."

I caught on. "You don't mean mine!" I gasped.

He did. "Don't you *see*? You might just be able to swing it. You know what your dad's like; he's so absentminded that half the time he doesn't really take in what you ask him, he just mutters something like 'Mmmf.' You ask him, he says 'Mmmf' and then you've got permission to use the car, or at least to sit in the car while Skull uses it to take us all to Scutchthorpe."

"But, but—"

He didn't even hear me; his pale blue eyes were lit with some kind of visionary gleam, the expression one saw in Irma Doone's eyes as she scribbled away in her poetry notebook. Creativity. "And your folks won't need the car," he babbled, "because they don't go anywhere much. Your dad can catch the bus to the University if he wants to go there; it's only fifteen minutes' walk to the bus stop, perhaps a bit more in your dad's case. And he won't notice it's missing, he'll think your Mum's got it."

"Yeah, what about Mum?"

"She mightn't notice it was gone either. She only takes it for the shopping and to go to the library. She hates shopping, and the library's closed in January."

It was a total fantasy. "Don't be crazy. Of course she'd notice. She'd think it was stolen and call the cops! We'd end up in jail somewhere."

Lou dropped down to earth. The crazed expression died out in his eyes and he gave a long, long sigh. "I guess you're right," he muttered.

"Even *my* parents aren't that far off the planet. Pretty far, but not far enough. Not when it comes to vanishing cars."

"Okay. But we could just *ask* your mother; she might be reasonable."

"Not when she hears who's doing the driving."

"Skull? Because of the stack, you mean?"

"The stack—and the other thing."

"What other thing? Oh, you mean—"

I nodded. "Yeah." A few weeks back, when Skull still had his wheels, there'd been a small misunderstanding. Mrs. Capsella had come in late from a visit to the library with a funny, haunted expression on her face. I didn't ask her what was wrong because I thought she'd probably discovered a couple of her own books for sale on the fifty-cent reject stall the librarians kept near the front desk, and it seemed the better part of valour to keep quiet. But after she'd gulped down a cup of coffee to steady her nerves, she'd told us that "some sort of barbarian" had chased her car for miles through the southeastern suburbs, blaring his horn and shouting at her through the open windows of his old Falcon. "He even knew my name!" she gasped. "He kept calling me Mrs. Capsella!"

It struck me at the time that it was an odd way for a barbarian to address a lady, but I didn't get the full truth of the matter until I saw Skull next day at school. He was feeling hurt. He told me he'd followed Mrs. Capsella for miles trying to warn her that she didn't have her lights switched on, but she hadn't taken a speck of notice and hadn't even thanked him for his trouble. "She could have been nabbed by the cops," he protested. "Failing to have your lights on at night is Dangerous Driving."

Mrs. Capsella said Skull was the one who could be had up for Dangerous Driving; she was sure he'd had his head out of the passenger window, and his arms weren't long enough to still be on the steering wheel.

"There's no way she'd let Skull drive us anywhere after that," I said. "Not even to the corner shop. Especially not in our car."

"Yeah," sighed Lou. He brightened a little. "We can still go by ourselves," he said. "There must be a train or something."

As it turned out later, there was something. There was the Celestial Omnibus.

■ ■ ■

When I got back from Lou's place, Mrs. Capsella was waiting for me in the kitchen. "I've washed all your summer clothes ready for Scutchthorpe," she announced with an ominous cheerfulness. "I even used the tennis ball."

Mrs. Capsella wasn't very talented in the laundry department. (She always wore black herself.) A brand-new garment, passing through her hands, came out looking like something dragged from the very bottom of a charity bin. I didn't want to arrive in Scutchthorpe looking like a reject, so I'd passed on this washing hint one of the girls at school had given me: that a tennis ball in the washing machine really makes things happen.

"Funny," observed Mrs. Capsella, indicating a heap of draggled clothing scattered on the couch. "It doesn't really look all that much different; it's just a khaki colour instead of that dark grey you don't like. Is that how it's supposed to be? Were you after the military look?"

Her face was utterly serious; that was the real pain of it, that she wasn't even trying to be funny. At that moment I felt I could have answered Mrs. Slewt's vacation essay in six words, if the bottom limit hadn't been fifteen hundred. "Why Do Birds Fly South in Winter?"—metaphorically or not, the answer was obvious: "To Get Away from Their Mothers."

"Not exactly," I replied. "What kind of tennis ball did you use, Mum?"

"It's over there." She pointed to something sitting in the middle of the kitchen bench, the sort of something that would have had the Health Department down on her in a flash if she'd been running a restaurant. (No chance of that; she poisoned only the family.) The object was mud coloured and soggy looking, with a ridge of chewed hair standing up on one end.

"Where'd you get that?"

"I found it in the Reserve."

Where some health-conscious German shepherd had wisely abandoned it, I thought bitterly. "You're supposed to use a new one," I explained. "From the Sports Store."

"Sports Store?" She looked at me blankly.

"They sell new ones there. You know, clean ones."

"Do they?" She smiled at me tolerantly, as if I was a four-year-old chattering on about fairies in the bottom of the garden. "Never mind. If the khaki isn't what you wanted, it will probably wash out, eventually."

Not if she had a hand in it, I thought. "Don't worry about it," I muttered.

"I wasn't."

"Well, just don't touch those clothes again, Mum. I'll take them to the launderette. Now, in fact." I bundled what had once been a fine summer wardrobe into an economy-sized garbage bag.

Mrs. Capsella followed me out to the front gate. "Do you want the tennis ball?" she asked.

"No thanks. Better throw it out and wash your hands, Mum."

I sloped off down the street, my pockets heavy with loose change for the machines. *Jingle jingle jingle*. There I was, trudging along, a gigantic sack over my shoulder, just a couple of weeks before Christmas. Sure enough, halfway down Silver Street a little kid poked his head up over a fence.

"Hiya, Santa Claus!" he said.

5

*T*he bus for Scutchthorpe left the terminal at six thirty. It was six fifteen when we arrived. We'd been held up at the railway exit because Lou had got his surfboard jammed in the turnstile. The ticket collector just stood and watched grimly from the other side, as if he thought we'd stuck the thing in there with the malicious intent of vandalising railway property. When we finally got it out and handed in our tickets, he let us walk on for a few yards before he called us back.

"That'll be four dollars eighty," he said.

"Four eighty! What for?"

"Two more tickets."

"For what?"

He jabbed a finger at our surfboards; we hadn't known they travelled full fare, like people. Lou tried to make a joke with the guy; he said his board should go half-fare because it was only two weeks old and would sit in his lap the whole time. The ticket collector had no sense of humour. He brought his big bushy eyebrows together in a single straight line so that he looked like he had a black bandanna wound round his forehead. "You kids want a fine?" he asked. I shoved five dollars at him fast before Lou got hysterical and asked, "A fine what?"

There were plenty of buses at the terminal, but not a single one had SCUTCHTHORPE on its destination board. As we humped our gear from bus to bus, the minutes ticking away fast on the big electric clock above the enquiry desk, I felt glad we'd managed to persuade the Capsellas to see us off at the local railway station. This was the kind of situation where Mrs. Capsella would have flown into such a noisy panic that I'd have leapt on any bus that was actually moving just to get away from her.

"We'd better ask someone," suggested Lou.

"Like who?" I replied, glancing towards the empty enquiry desk.

"Those guys." Lou pointed to two drivers leaning against the side of a big Brisbane-bound Greyhound. I'd noticed them several times as we scampered about the yard, watching us and grinning to each other as if we were some kind of act from Free Entertainment in the Parks.

"They look like the kind of guys who wouldn't tell a lost three-year-old where to find his mother," I said.

"But the bus is going to go in *five* minutes!" wailed Lou.

Click! went the big clock up on the wall, knocking off one more; it seemed to be the only thing working round the place. "Okay, okay." I hitched at my rucksack, which was biting savagely into my shoulder blades, and we fronted up to the two guys.

"Do you know where the Scutchthorpe bus goes from?" I asked.

They looked us over silently before they answered. At sixteen, I'd been a teenager for four years and you get used to this kind of treatment. Little kids and adults get answers right away; teenagers have to wait till they've been looked over.

"Scutchthorpe?" enquired the taller driver, eyeing my

surfboard, which seemed to amuse him. "You kids don't look like you come from Scutchthorpe."

"We didn't come from—" I began, but he cut me off, turning to his mate.

"Don't look like they come from Scutchthorpe, do they, Mick?"

Mick shook his head and spat a wad of gum halfway across the bus park. "Nope," he replied. "They sure don't."

"We don't *come* from Scutchthorpe," explained Lou. "We're *going* there."

"*Going* there? You're going to Scutchthorpe?"

"Any reason why we shouldn't?"

Mick unwrapped a fresh stick of gum. "No reason at all." He eyed our surfboards. "Been on holidays?"

"No, we're *going* on holidays." Just then the big clock lopped off another minute and Lou's nerves broke. "Please, please, can you tell us where the Scutchthorpe bus goes from?" he pleaded.

"Sure, sonny." Mick straightened to attention and flicked a speck of dust from the collar of his jacket. "Sure thing." He waved towards the farthest corner of the terminal, a deserted spot beyond a wide grass verge. "Over there."

"That's the Scutchthorpe bus?" we gasped.

"Right on," said Mick.

We'd seen that bus several times during our search, but we hadn't bothered to check out its destination board for the simple reason that it didn't look mobile. It was so old-fashioned we'd taken it for a kind of kiddy play fixture. We humped our stuff across the grass verge and stared up at the destination board. " 'Yarrabung,' " wondered Lou.

"We'd better ask." I was fed up with asking drivers, but Yarrabung didn't sound like the kind of place you'd want to land in by mistake. I eased off my rucksack, dumped it on the ground, and climbed the bus steps; they were corrugated metal ones like you get on escalators, with blobs of ancient chewing gum stuck down the grooves.

"Does this bus go to Scutchthorpe?"

The guy behind the steering wheel peered at me over the top of his racing guide. "You want to go to Scutchthorpe?"

"Yeah. Does this bus go there?"

"Does if you want it to."

"Um, what does that mean?"

"It means it goes through Scutchthorpe and I'll stop and let you off if you really want to go there. Do you?"

"Yes. Er, do you think you could open the baggage compartment so we could put our stuff in?"

"Baggage compartment?" He gave a dry bark of laughter that was echoed faintly by an old man sitting in the front seat. "We don't have a baggage compartment, son. Just the racks; that do you?"

"Racks?" For a crazy, disoriented second I actually thought he was talking about medieval torture equipment.

"Yeah, racks." He turned round and pointed upwards.

Along the wall above the seats was a line of narrow wooden shelves. No hope of getting our gear up there, and even if that was possible, you could bet it wouldn't stay put. "Is it okay if we leave our stuff on one of the empty seats?"

"Take your pick." He went back to his racing guide.

There were certainly plenty of vacant seats; apart from the old man at the front there were only two other passengers on the bus, a lady and a little kid. A giant holdall, almost as big as a person, crouched on the floor beside the lady's seat, and as we passed Lou got the end of his surfboard caught through its handles. The holdall lurched slowly along the floor as if it was crawling after him, and straightaway the little kid started screaming.

"Mum! Mum! That boy's pinching our bag!"

The lady didn't take all that much notice at first; she had a pencil in her hand and was filling in the answers to a magazine quiz. As I bent down to help Lou, I couldn't help catching a glimpse of the title over her shoulder: "Are You Lovable?" The lady may have been, but the little kid certainly wasn't. "Mum! Mum!" He tugged at her arm. "They're pinching our *bag!*"

The lady glanced up, looked us over briefly, and turned back to the kid. "Trevor," she said in a tired voice, "cut out that racket."

"But Mu-um, they're pinching—"

She looked him straight in the eye. "Trevor, do you want us to get off this bus and go back and have another holiday at Granny's place?"

Trevor went quiet. We freed the surfboard and Lou laid it carefully on a spare seat next to mine. "Do you think we need tickets for them?" I whispered.

"Could be. I'll go and ask him." He wandered down the aisle towards the driver. "Do we need tickets for the boards?" he asked.

"Tickets for the *boards*?" The driver raised his eyebrows and winked across at the old man, the sort of wink that says: "Look what I've got here!"

"Yeah, to—to take them on the bus."

"You can buy them tickets if you want to, sonny." He grinned. "You can buy them anything you like: icy poles, a packet of crisps—take them to the pictures on Saturday night, do you?"

"I just wanted to be certain," said Lou stiffly.

"Sure you did." The driver winked again at his elderly companion.

It was too good a joke for him to forget; five minutes later as we lurched out through the gates he called back over his shoulder: "If your board wants to visit the restroom, son, just give me a shout and I'll pull over right away!"

■ ■ ■

Over the Westgate Bridge, through the last straggling suburbs and the city was left behind, just a line of towers and a pall of blue-grey smoke on the far edge of a summer sky.

Lou let out a long sigh. "I can't believe we've really made it!" he exclaimed. His voice echoed loudly along the bus; three pairs of eyes turned to stare at him, and the driver's neck twitched above the rim of his bus company shirt collar. The little kid clambered out of his seat and came to stand next to ours, staring, his round eyes resting on our faces like a pair of sticky lollipops.

"Trevor!" called his mother. "Come back here and sit down, please." Trevor ambled back to his seat, climbed up on it, and gazed at us some more.

"Those boys are *funny*!" he told his mum.

He couldn't have been more than four years old, but he made you feel uncomfortable. How did we appear to him? What did he mean by "funny"? Did he mean comical; did we make him laugh? Or did he mean peculiar, like there was something wrong with us? I found myself glancing down to check if my sweatshirt was back-to-front, or the zipper of my jeans undone. If I'd been in the habit of carrying a mirror in my pocket, I might have checked up on my face.

"Trevor, turn around, please. Don't gawp at people!"

"But they're *funny*!"

"I don't care how funny they are, it's none of your business. Don't gawp!" Trevor's head vanished with a jerky abruptness that suggested the disappearance wasn't entirely voluntary.

"Here, eat this and be quiet." There was a slow, faint rustle of Glad Wrap. From the kid's disappointed squawk I figured he'd been given some kind of sandwich. "Yuck! I don't want *that*!"

"Just *eat* it!"

A sorry squelching noise filled the bus, and suddenly I remembered Mrs. Capsella's remark about Scutchthorpe: "Awful name—reminds you of soggy toast crusts glugging down a sinkhole."

Lou closed his eyes. The old man got out of his place and headed for the long seat at the back, where he stretched out full-length and settled down to sleep. Outside the window, paddocks and sheep whizzed by, and the odd farmhouse, but there was no sign of the sea. Soon the sky began to darken, the old man began to snore, and like Lou, I closed my eyes.

■ ■ ■

When I woke, it was dark outside. I checked my watch: nine thirty-five; I figured we must be getting close to Scutchthorpe. The man at the Tourist Bureau had told Mrs. Capsella the bus arrived there at ten o'clock. Like Lou, I couldn't quite believe we'd actually *made* it; that we'd got away, out on our own for a whole week. And when the bus slowed beside a level crossing and the headlights of a car crept up behind, I had this sudden crazy fear that the Capsellas had followed us, that they'd hold up the bus and collect us like a pair of runaway toddlers. But the car turned off harmlessly along a small side road and the bus lumbered on towards Scutchthorpe.

The problem, I decided, was the way Lou and I saw ourselves: deep in our hearts we just didn't think we were the kind of kids who went raging in places like Scutchthorpe. Perhaps the holiday would cure us of that; it might, I thought, even cure Lou of this other little problem he had, being scared of girls. It might even cure me.

Not that I was really scared of them; some of my best friends were girls—it was just that all the stuff Broadside Williams had told us about making out with girls on the beach had made me feel slightly apprehensive. I mean, Broadside was talking about girls he'd never even met before! I couldn't imagine making out with someone who was practically a total stranger. It seemed bizarre, a bit like those horror movies where everything seems perfectly normal and peaceful and ordinary and then *wham*— suddenly this clawlike hand, blood dripping from its talons, comes reaching out of the wall. Perhaps Scutchthorpe would cure me of this idea, an idea I knew Broadside would describe as a "hang-up." Perhaps I'd become more—well, "laid back," another phrase he used.

I glanced at Lou. He was one person it was really difficult to imagine getting "laid back." He clammed up if a girl started talking to him when he was standing by himself in the playground at recess, even if she was someone he'd known since kindergarten. But you never knew what might happen in a place like Scutchthorpe, I told myself. Broadside had said the female population there outnumbered the male three to one, and with those kind of figures it was just possible Lou might come across a girl who was a bit like himself. A nervous girl who liked weird conversations. They'd be so busy exchanging worries that they'd get closer and closer without even noticing; they might even accidentally slide into each other's arms—unconsciously, like they were having a mental blackout, or even some kind of fit. And that would give them something more to worry and talk about; they'd never be at a loss for conversation.

Yeah, he could get cured that way. It was hard to imagine that type of nervous, shy girl going to a place like Scutchthorpe, but then in the ordinary run of things you wouldn't expect a boy like Lou to be there either. Perhaps the shy girl's folks had a holiday house like Bilbar, and she might have a normal friend who'd suggested they go somewhere else together—yeah, she might have a friend like that, a really great girl . . .

Lou began to stir. He gave a little grunt, yawned, and slowly opened his eyes. He stared at the seat in front of him as if he didn't quite know where he was, then he turned his head and looked out the window, but all he saw there was the reflection of his own face, staring back from the dark glass. He shuddered, then turned round and saw me. "What's the time?"

"Nine forty-five. Should be there in fifteen minutes."

"Nine forty-five," he repeated. "That's, uh, ten forty-five, no, wait a minute, that's twelve forty-five in Stockholm."

"Stockholm?"

"Yeah, It's in Sweden, it's the capital. And it's twelve forty-five in the afternoon there, because there's nine hours' time difference."

Before I could ask him why he thought I'd be interested

in what time it was in Stockholm, or even why *he* was interested, he'd twisted round and was groping about in the seat behind, searching for something in his rucksack. It was a camera.

"Oh, great! I forgot mine."

"I forgot my watch." He paused. "I was wondering—" He caught his lower lip between his teeth and started chewing on it. For some reason he glanced towards the window again, and his reflection stared right back like some kind of monster pursuing the vehicle. It upset him. "Do you think I'm weird looking?" he blurted.

It can be pretty awful when someone throws a question at you that's entirely unexpected. The subject didn't surprise me; I knew Lou was deeply worried about his looks. It had started way back when he was seven and Mr. Santini at the pizza shop had told him he was a funny-looking kid. Mr. Santini said this kind of thing to lots of people; I guess he got bored slapping pizzas round all day and liked to see shock bloom on his customers' faces. And you could never convince Lou that Mr. Santini hadn't been right on target in his particular case. But knowing all this didn't prepare me for Lou suddenly throwing the question at me on the Scutchthorpe bus, and I said the first thing that came into my mind. "Yes, you are," I answered, and then hastily added: "Just a bit."

It was hard to figure exactly why Lou was weird looking; sometimes I thought it was simply that he worried about it so much that we'd all come to take it for a fact. Then again, the first time my grandmother set eyes on him she'd said, "You're certainly no oil painting, are you?"

Lou was shortish all right, but not short enough for little kids to point at him in the street. There was nothing wrong with his face when you thought about it in detail; all his features were an ordinary size and shape and in the normal places. The one thing that did make him look strange, I guess, was his paleness. He had that very white skin red-haired people have, only he didn't have red hair—it was just an ordinary pale brown shade. His eyes were very pale too, a washed-out, faded blue. My grandfather Neddy Blount, who wasn't as rude as his wife, called him "that little bloke who always looks as if he's just seen a ghost."

I stumbled on. "I mean, you look weird in that window reflection, but so do I, so would anyone. It's an effect of light or something."

"You needn't bother to cover up. I can recognise the truth when I hear it," he said bitterly.

"No, honest, you're okay. The only thing wrong with your looks, *really*, is that you're always so pale. When you get a bit of a tan at Scutchthorpe, you'll look fine."

"Think so?" he asked eagerly. "Generally I just go red as a lobster, and then scaly, like some kind of reptile." He jiggled with the camera on his lap. "Do you think that in a photograph, a black-and-white one, the red would show up like a tan?"

"Dunno. I guess it might."

"Do you think you'd be able to take a photo of me so I come out looking all right?"

"I'll try—sorry, I mean, sure thing."

"Great." He settled back in his seat. "What's the time now?"

"Nine fifty."

"Nine fifty." He smiled to himself. "Twelve fifty in Stockholm."

What was he on about? Somehow I didn't like to ask, and one thing I knew about Lou. If he had something on his mind, good or bad, you'd get to know about it eventually.

"We should be there in ten minutes," I said.

But twenty minutes passed and we were still rattling along the highway.

"How long till Scutchthorpe?" I called to the driver.

"Not all that long. You boys going to Adelaide?"

Adelaide? "We're going to Scutchthorpe," I reminded him. "How come you thought we were going to Adelaide? Does this bus go to Adelaide on the way to, um, Yarrabung?"

"Nope. But the bus to Adelaide goes past Scutchthorpe round midnight. Thought you boys might be planning to flag it down."

"No," I said firmly. "We're going to Scutchthorpe."

"That so? Been on holiday?"

"No. *Why do these guys keep thinking we've just been on holiday?*" I whispered to Lou.

He didn't answer. I don't think he'd even heard; he was peering all round the bus with a panicky look in his eyes, as if he'd just discovered something very wrong. "Hey!" he squeaked. "Where are those other people: the old man, and the lady with the little kid?"

"I don't know. They must have got off somewhere while we were asleep."

"Got off? But how come we didn't see them?"

"I told you, we were asleep."

"But wouldn't we have woken up when the bus stopped?"

I shrugged. "Not if we were really sound asleep."

He leaned towards me. "Could you *be* that sound asleep?"

"Sure. I don't know about you, but I was dead beat from lugging our stuff around. We probably wouldn't have noticed if the bus had gone over a cliff."

He sank back in his seat, frowning. "I suppose so." We rattled on some more. Beside me, I could feel Lou boiling up, like he does when he gets some weird idea in his head and it starts to take over. He's like milk creeping slowly up the sides of a pot, then *wham!* it spills right over.

He spilled over all right. Quietly at first, though, so that I didn't immediately figure what he was on about. "Have you ever read this story called 'The Celestial Omnibus'?" he asked.

"Don't think I've ever come across it. Was it in that short-story collection we had first semester? I didn't read the whole of that book, not after Mrs. Slewt said there wasn't going to be an exam question on it, so—"

He sighed. "You didn't read it. Okay, it doesn't matter, I'll tell you the story. There's this boy, see, and he finds this odd sort of bus stop down a blind alley near his house. It belongs to the Surbiton and Celestial Road Car Company, and the bus goes to, well—heaven. The boy doesn't believe this, of course, he thinks it's some kind of joke, but then he creeps out of his house one morning and takes the bus, and—"

"And?"

"It's empty, except for the driver." Lou glanced fearfully round the vacant seats of our own vehicle. "And the driver's weird; he talks in Latin all the time. So the kid gets scared and wants to get off, only the driver won't stop. And—and the bus *does* go to heaven—there's a great *gulf,* and an everlasting river." He shuddered. "I don't think I want to go to heaven."

"Not much chance of that."

He didn't smile. "What do you think of it?"

"The story?" I shrugged. "The guy who wrote it must have been a salt eater."

"A what?"

"A person who eats too much salt. He probably had pizza for supper and it gave him nightmares. Too much salt can do that."

"I don't think they had pizzas back then," said Lou stiffly. "Not in England, anyway."

"Was he English? Perhaps he ate a kipper, then."

"You're missing the *point*."

I grinned at him. "You sound like Mrs. Slewt. What is this, English Revision time?"

"But it's *not* the point. I'm not just talking about the story for fun, it's because—" He paused, glanced round again, and continued in a hoarse whisper. "Just take a close look round this thing, will you? Check out a few details. Those luggage racks, for instance. Now where have you seen those kind of racks before, except in some old black-and-white movie? And the windows actually *open*— look, there's little grooves to fit your fingers in!"

"Geez, I wish I'd known that; it's suffocating in here. Give us a go!" I leaned across him, fitted my fingers in the groove, and tugged at the pane. The window didn't budge; it was gummed shut with dust and age. Lou shoved me back to my side of the seat. "Where's Yarrabung?" he hissed in my ear.

"Yarrabung?"

"The name on the front of the bus. Have you ever heard of it?"

"Nope. It's probably some little dump way out in the country. A terminus or something."

"A terminus." He echoed the word hollowly. "Know what that means? The *end* of the line—like heaven, or hell. And it's not just funny we didn't hear those people get off; do you realise we didn't see them *get on?*"

"How could we? We were late, remember? They were already there, inside."

"Already there, or"—he spoke the next words in the slow, deep voice used by the hosts of midnight horror shows—"or *not* there?"

"What?"

He slapped his forehead with the back of his hand. "Don't you get it yet? A bus going to nowhere, an old bus that looks like it came from another world, passengers who vanish, or who weren't really there in the first place. And have a good look at the driver's face—see those sunken eyes, that terrifying jaw?"

"Come off it! He'd have trouble getting a job in a Coke ad, I'll admit, but he's not—hey!" I broke off in astonishment, suddenly getting his drift. Perhaps it was the weird way Lou thought that made him seem so weird looking, I decided. Sometimes I wake up at three in the morning with some pretty strange ideas myself. They seem real at the time, but they don't when I'm pouring milk on my cornflakes five hours later. The trouble with Lou was that for him it was always three o'clock in the morning, and dark outside. "You don't *really* think this is the Celestial Omnibus, do you?" I gasped.

He nodded.

"Give us a break! That's just some wanky yarn they set for year-eleven English. It's not *real.*"

"There's just us," moaned Lou. "And him." He nodded

towards the driver's hulking back. "Pretty soon now he's going to turn round and start talking to us in Latin."

"Geez, I don't think he'll do that; he was reading the *Turf Guide* back at the terminal."

The bus gave a great rattling shudder and lurched to a halt. The driver turned. There *was* something a bit terrifying about his jaw, I thought shakily. His mouth opened and we sat there, frozen to our seats, waiting for him to speak.

"Scutchthorpe!" bawled the driver.

6

■

*W*e were standing on the edge of an empty road, dark paddocks stretching away on either side. Off in the distance, now almost out of sight, the red taillights of the bus grew small as pinpricks and then vanished altogether. Jolting along those last few miles, with Lou panicking beside me, I'd felt I'd never be so happy as when I saw the back of that bus, but as those red pinpricks disappeared I felt pinpricks in myself—of fright. Something, I thought, looking out over the lightless paddocks, was definitely wrong.

"Why is it so dark?" said Lou.

"Yeah, I was just wondering that myself. Broadside said the place was bright as noon at four o'clock in the morning." An image of the bus driver's face as he watched us stumble down the steps with our gear flashed into my mind. The grin that parted his tombstone teeth had been definitely diabolical, though not in the sense that Lou had imagined. "That jerk's left us way out of town," I said. "He must take a turn-off before he hits Scutchthorpe, so he's just dumped us here. The town must be up the road." A long way up, I thought.

Lou grabbed at my arm. "Look! Look at that—that *thing* over there!"

"What thing?"

"That white *figure*," he gibbered. "Can't you see? It's

got its arms stretched out, as if it's welcoming us. I can't look, I can't look anymore." He covered his eyes with one arm. "Don't *look* at it, Al, it's—"

"A ghost?" I saw what had caught his attention. Lou was a bit shortsighted; he should have had glasses years ago, only he figured they'd make him even more weird looking. "Bit on the thin side, isn't it? I don't think ghosts suffer from anorexia."

"Don't *look* at it; it's better not to catch their eyes. Once you catch their eyes, you're done for."

"Done for, eh?" I strode across to the white "figure" and read the message held in its outstretched arms. Then I strode back to Lou, grabbed his arm, and began pulling him across the road. He pulled back, shielding his eyes with the other arm. "Let go!" he squeaked. "What're you doing? Have you gone crazy?"

"No, you have." Mercilessly, I dragged him to the edge of the road and placed his trembling hand fair and square on the splintery wood of the old signpost. "Feel that? Pretty substantial, eh? Ever come across a wooden ghost before?"

His arm dropped down from his eyes. "Oh, yeah," he said sheepishly. "Hey, look, it says 'Welcome to Scutchthorpe.' At least we know which direction to take now. It's up the road, not down." He peered doubtfully ahead into the darkness. "But shouldn't we be able to see it from here? I mean, the lights?"

"Sometimes they put those signs miles out of town."

"Yeah, but—"

I cut him short. I wasn't feeling too happy myself. I was feeling, well, *young*, and as we trudged on up the road, passing more empty paddocks and only one unlighted cottage, I began feeling younger and younger, so young that if we'd come across a telephone box I feared I might have slipped inside and rung up the Capsellas. Such an idea would have been unbelievable just twelve hours back when I was safe in my home and dying to get away from it. I imagined my voice whingeing down the telephone wire: "Help, we're lost!"—I imagined Mrs. Capsella's gasp of alarm and, perhaps, of satisfaction; all those years of watchdoggery had not been in vain. "Have some self-respect," I muttered to myself.

"What?" asked Lou.

"Nothing," I mumbled. "I just said, 'Lots of insects about.' "

We plodded on doggedly past another stretch of empty paddocks, and at last a gleam of light shone up ahead. Only a gleam, nothing like the festive blaze we'd expected, and when we reached the source we found nothing more than a small cluster of buildings by the roadside. If you can call four buildings a cluster. Mrs. Slewt sometimes asked questions like that in English: "How many swallows make a summer?" for instance. I'd always felt they had no relation to real life at all; now I saw dimly that they might be relevant. Could you call four buildings—a general store, a boarded-up Tea Shoppe, a feedstore, a bank—a town? Could you even call it Scutchthorpe? I wondered, my heart sinking. No, it couldn't be; we had to be in the wrong place.

Lou was peering at the sign on the door of the general store. " 'Terence Finnegan, Proprietor,' " he read. The door was closed, but there was a light behind it, the lone glimmer we'd seen from down the road. "Is this *it*?" he whispered, turning his broad pale face towards me. "Is this Scutchthorpe?"

"Of course it's not. It couldn't be, could it?" I said in a

firm voice. "I mean, look for yourself, there's no, uh, discos." The word sounded frail, tacky as old tinsel, and as I spoke it an owl hooted out of the night.

"The Scutchthorpe Band," said Lou bleakly.

"It must be farther up the road," I said. "The town, I mean."

"What's this then?"

I shrugged. "Just a couple of shops on the outskirts."

We soldiered on, past another stretch of paddocks, another unlighted cottage, and a little farther on, an old-fashioned telephone box that looked like the one in *Dr. Who*. I steeled myself against its homely light, the comfort of familiar voices on the end of the line. Lou glanced toward it longingly. "Do you think we should, er, ring up?" he suggested.

"Who?" I asked. "Who did you have in mind?"

He flushed, and I knew he was thinking of giving his own folks a buzz. Or rather, as the Cadigorns had no telephone at Bilbar, giving one to mine. "Uh, no one," he mumbled.

A little farther on we came to a white weatherboard house. A faint blue light flickered behind its front windows. Someone was watching television, someone was *in* there, and at this obvious sign of life I felt a surge of relief, which ended abruptly as we came upon another WELCOME TO SCUTCHTHORPE signpost, this one facing round the other way.

"Well, that's it," exclaimed Lou. "That *was* Scutchthorpe."

"It can't be," I said weakly.

"Because there's no discos?"

"Because there's no anything. Broadside Williams said—"

"Broadside Williams!" Lou flung his surfboard down on the grass beside the road, unhitched his rucksack, and cast himself down on it. "Has it ever struck you that Broadside was a bit prone to exaggeration?"

"Sure it has—but not this kind of exaggeration. Look, if Broadside was going out with a girl who was fairly good-looking he'd rave on about her like she was Miss Australia, wouldn't he? But if he was going out with a real dog, what did he do then?"

Lou shrugged. A wounded expression appeared on his face. "I don't think you should judge girls—or any-body—in terms of their physical appearance," he said stiffly.

"Of course not. I don't, but Broadside did. And what would he do if he *was* going out with a—a plain sort of girl? He'd keep quiet about it, wouldn't he? And so, if he took a holiday in a real dump, he'd keep quiet about that, too—he wouldn't say a word. He wouldn't go on about what a raging joint it was, just in case some kid from school happened to come here, and find out."

Lou pondered. "I don't know about that. He might think no one would ever come here. Or he might figure *they'd* keep quiet, think they'd made a mistake—or he mightn't give a hang either way."

I slid my hand into my pocket and something crackled reassuringly. All at once I felt fine. "*I know* we're not in Scutchthorpe," I said triumphantly. "I've got proof!"

"Like what?"

"Look around. Do you see anything that looks like a hol-iday apartment block, or a set of units?"

Lou snickered faintly. The sort of low, exhausted snicker you might give if an elderly great-uncle was reading you the entire contents of *The Golden Treasury of Children's Humour* and had just reached the very last page.

"Right! You don't see any units, and that means"—I drew the crumpled wad of paper from my pocket and waved it in front of his nose—"that means this can't be Scutchthorpe."

"How do you figure that?"

"Kooka Kabins, of course. Mum booked us in at the Tourist Bureau, and if the Kabins aren't here, then obviously this can't be the real Scutchthorpe."

"The *real* Scutchthorpe? What do you mean? You mean this is a kind of hallucination?"

"I mean this is the *old* town. There must be a bypass or something and this is the old part that got left behind, and the new one"—I waved across the paddocks—"is out there somewhere, near the sea. You know how those old seaside towns were built a mile or so inland, near the highway. The new place, the resort town, is probably right smack on the beach. We'll just have to go back to that store and find someone to ask. There was a light on, so they must be still up."

Someone was still up; the door of the store was standing open and a small pear-shaped man, in shorts and a white T-shirt with *Aloha!* printed on the front, was putting his cat out for the night. Mr. Finnegan, I guessed.

"You boys looking for the bus to Adelaide?" he enquired. "Bus stop's about a mile down the road, just past the signpost. Surprised Bert didn't let you know when he dropped you off. Came on the Yarrabung bus, didn't you?"

"Yeah, but we're not going to Adelaide."

The cat jumped out of Mr. Finnegan's arms and settled

down on the footpath. It blinked up at our surfboards, its lips parted in a wide Cheshire grin.

"We're looking"—Lou darted an uneasy glance at me—"for Scutchthorpe."

Mr. Finnegan put his head on one side, and the grin he gave us was as wide and sly as his cat's. "You're innit, mate."

"Yeah, we saw the signposts. We're looking for the new town."

"Newtown?" Mr. Finnegan shook his head. "No place of that name round here. There's Weeba, about fifty kilometres up the highway, and Uloola, due east. No Newtown, though. Only Newtown I know's in Sydney; got a cousin living there."

"Not Newtown," explained Lou. "New town—two words."

"The newer part of Scutchthorpe," I put in.

"Nothing much new round here," replied Mr. Finnegan. "No, wait a minute, I'm telling you a lie. There's a fancy new house up along the Uloola Road, about five miles past the fork. Bloke from the city built it for a holiday house, came one summer with the family and hasn't been back since. Is that what you're looking for? You relatives of his or something?"

"No, it's not one house, Mr. Finnegan, it's a whole *place*." Lou's voice had taken on a thin, desperate note. "A kind of holiday town, with hotels and apartments and—and discos."

"Discos?" echoed Mr. Finnegan wonderingly.

"They're places where you go to dance, and, and—"

Mr. Finnegan flapped his hand to and fro beside his ear, as if he was fanning up a cool breeze. "See that?" he asked. "No straw hanging out of *my* ears, sonny. I know what a disco is, don't you worry. But there's nothing like that round here, and if anyone told you different they've been pulling your leg." He glanced down at his cat. "Eh, Tib?"

"Yeah," muttered Lou. "And we know who *that* was." I whisked the piece of paper from my pocket. "Actually, Mr. Finnegan, we're looking for Kooka Kabins," I explained.

"Kooka Kabin!" Mr. Finnegan's grin became human. "Why didn't you say so in the first place? That's different, then. You're looking for Mrs. Mulroony's place. Girls sent you, did they?"

Lou's voice trembled slightly. "What girls?"

"Mrs. Mulroony's lot. They're up in Surfers for the holidays. You friends of theirs, then?"

"No." There was something a bit wrong with this guy, I decided. He was slow to catch on, or else he seemed to be catching on to an entirely different conversation, one that he might be having in his head, perhaps. I spoke my next words very slowly and deliberately, with long spaces in between, like some of the teachers did when they were explaining a little matter to Cherry Clagg. "We're looking for Kooka Kabins," I repeated. "Main Road, Scutchthorpe."

"So you said, son." Mr. Finnegan's eyes glinted sharply and when he went on, his voice was equally slow and deliberate, as if he thought I was some kind of idiot. "Kooka Kabin, that's Mrs. Mulroony's. She runs the place. Got it now, have you? You'll find her up at the White House, near the edge of town—the way you guys came in from just now. You must have passed right by it." He cocked his head on one side again. "Mrs. Mulroony expecting you?"

"We had a reservation."

"Reservation, eh?" He gave a low cackle.

"I mean, my mum fixed up the booking," I said.

"Oh, well, that's okay, then; Mrs. Mulroony'll be expecting you. Just knock on the door. Might have to do it a few times; she likes the TV loud. Tell her Terry sent you."

We shouldered our rucksacks and picked up our surfboards again. Mr. Finnegan went inside his store and closed the door. A moment later the single light in Old Scutchthorpe was extinguished. The cat blinked at us solemnly from the footpath.

■ ■ ■

The faint strains of *Advance Australia Fair* came drifting over the White House lawn as we stumbled up the front path.

"Television's shutting down," muttered Lou. "Must be pretty late. What time is it?"

"Three o'clock in Stockholm," I muttered. The strap of my rucksack was biting savagely again, and my new running shoes had worn a fiery blister in my heel.

Lou acted like he didn't hear, or perhaps his attention had been distracted by the sight of a face peering at us through the curtains of the front window. "Do you think this Mrs. Mulroony will drive us out to Kooka Kabins?" he asked. "Or are we going to have to trudge—"

Before he could finish, the front door of the White House burst open and a burly lady in a bright pink dressing gown hallooed into the yard. "Captain Cellar!" she called, peering through the darkness. "Captain Cellar?"

"Must be calling her cat in," I whispered.

"Funny name for a cat."

The burly lady came down the steps, her pink gown billowing out behind her. There was a friendly, welcoming expression on her face, but as she came closer it changed to one of uncertainty, and then suspicion. "What are you kids doing here?" she demanded.

"The man at the store told us to tell you Terry sent us," I said quickly. "I'm Al Capsella, and this is Louis Cadigorn. We're the people who booked into Kooka Kabins for the week. I'm sorry we're late, but we got a bit—lost."

Mrs. Mulroony seemed puzzled. "Mr. Pinkle at the Tourist Bureau didn't say anything to me about two kids being in the party," she said doubtfully. "He said a couple; I understood Captain and Mrs. Cellar were coming on their own." She sighed. "I doubt if there'll be space in there for the four of you, though it's quite roomy, mind. I'll see what I can fix up for you—there's a couple of old cots out the back somewhere." She waved a hand vaguely over the White House and added in a more kindly tone: "Nothing worse than a holiday gone wrong at the start, is there?"

The words seemed to hang in the air, ominously, in the slight pause before Mrs. Mulroony rushed on. "I remember the time poor Alf and I and the three kiddies went off to the Gold Coast one Christmas. Donkey's years ago, it was; Tracey was still in nappies. Some bloke Alf met passing through Uloola told him there was no need for us to book if we were going up the Gold Coast; said the place was full of empty flats all year round, even at Christmas." She sighed gustily. "You wouldn't credit it! We ended up in a caravan park, and we didn't have no caravan, neither. Rained the whole fortnight and we had to get a bus to the beach, it was that far away. The girls were disappointed, I can tell you, and poor Alf got crook with the water. He was always delicate that way, poor soul; it did for him in the end." She flashed us a teary smile. "Well, you boys didn't come all this way to hear about other people's holidays, did you? Funny, though, I could have sworn Mr. Pinkle at the Bureau told me—"

"My mother made the booking," I said. "There must have been some sort of misunderstanding."

"Your mother, dear? The Captain's wife?"

"There isn't any Captain, Mrs. Mulroony," I explained. "That's just my surname, and my mother's and father's. Mr. and Mrs. Capsella, like Mr. and Mrs. Smith—"

"Or Mr. and Mrs. Sergeant," snickered Lou.

"Oh. And this Mr. and Mrs. Sergeant, they're coming on later tonight, are they? I'm not *quite* sure where those old cots are, to tell you the truth. I haven't laid eyes on them since Alf passed away, he used them to put up his poker mates now and again, but I'm pretty sure I'll be able to rustle something up for you."

"There's no Mr. and Mrs. Sergeant, Mrs. Mulroony," I said, glaring at Lou. "My parents aren't coming. There's just us; we're having a holiday on our own."

"A holiday on your own?" Mrs. Mulroony looked as if she'd never heard of such a thing. "What, away from your family, dear?" She clucked her tongue loudly. "There's nothing like a nice family holiday, I always say. I said it to the girls last November, but they didn't take a speck of notice. Come December, they upped and went." A sudden suspicion gleamed in Mrs. Mulroony's eyes. "Your parents know you're here, don't they?" she asked sharply.

"Sure, Mrs. Mulroony, no worries. You can ring them if you like. I'll give you the number."

"Oh, I'm sure that won't be necessary, dear. Still, you can give it to me just in case. Tomorrow morning will do. Better safe than sorry, isn't it?" She smiled at us. "I can see you're a couple of well-brought-up boys. My! You're all dressed up, aren't you? Look like something off the television, the pair of you." We were wearing perfectly ordinary clothes. Ordinary for the kind of crowd we'd expected to find in Scutchthorpe, that is. In that sort of mob we'd have been exactly like everyone else, but here in Mrs. Mulroony's front yard I suddenly had the sense that we looked outlandish, even ridiculous. I gave my shorts a hitch, suddenly wishing they were Bermudas, like the ones Mr. Finnegan wore.

"Pity the girls aren't here," chirped Mrs. Mulroony.

"Girls?" asked Lou.

Mrs. Mulroony beamed. "My three. They'd have got a real kick out of seeing you. But they're up at Surfers—saved all year for the holidays, they did, wanted a taste of the bright lights." She spread her arms wide. "Well, I was disappointed, but you can't blame them, I suppose. You're only young once. Isn't it queer, though, how you two look like you've *come* from the bright lights, while my three—" She shook her head wonderingly. "Funny old world, isn't it?" Reaching deep into the pocket of her pink gown, Mrs. Mulroony drew out a bundle of keys. "Come on, then, I'll show you over to Kooka."

As we followed the solid pink back round the side of the White House, Lou whispered, "Is she going to drive us over in her dressing gown?"

"This is Scutchthorpe," I told him. "Anything goes. Besides, as long as she's not our mother it doesn't matter what she wears."

"Yeah!" Lou flashed me a big grin. He was feeling better, and so was I. Once we were out of here, roaring along the road to the New Scutchthorpe, this funny little nightmare would be forgotten. We'd had a bad start, that was all, and in half an hour it would all be behind us.

We skirted the back veranda of the White House, crossed a patch of stubby lawn, and headed towards the garage, a long, low shed with a slight lean to it. Mrs. Mulroony fitted her key into the door. It must be the side door, I figured, because it was far too narrow to drive a car through; you'd have had trouble with a motorcycle. The main door must be at the back.

Mrs. Mulroony was having trouble with the lock. "Bugger of a thing," she observed. "You have to get the knack of it, and it's been so long since we had anyone that I've forgotten. Never mind, you boys'll pick it up soon enough. Easy as pie, once you get the hang." She gave a final fumble and the narrow door lurched open. She reached up and switched on the light.

There wasn't a sign of a vehicle. It wasn't a garage. The light was murky, but in its evil glow I saw beige wallpaper with a pattern of sailing boats and dancing sailors, two sagging beds with pink chenille covers, an assortment of tatty chairs, and a thin-legged card table. With a choking gasp, Lou flung himself through the door and laid his hand on the edge of the table. *Wonka wonka wonka,* it said.

"Welcome to Kooka Kabin, boys!" cried Mrs. Mulroony.

7

When I opened my eyes that first morning in Scutchthorpe I didn't have a clue where I was or what day it was or even how old I was. Perhaps it was because I'd been dreaming. In the dream I was a little kid who'd bought a ticket with his own money to ride on the Elevated Railway. I didn't know what the Elevated Railway was, exactly, just that it was something so special I'd have given anything to have one single ride.

I couldn't find it. With the ticket clutched in my hand I raced up and down the streets, asking people if they knew where it was. They just stared at me blankly. "But I've got a ticket!" I kept shouting. "See? I bought it with my own money! And I'm old enough; it says 'minimum age six years'!" I was sweating all over when I struggled awake—and then I found myself staring at a row of sailing boats.

Sailing boats? Where was I? Beneath the boats was a row of dancing sailors and beneath them, more boats, more sailors. Wallpaper—and halfway up the wall was a funny kind of wooden shelf that looked a bit like a varnished chicken perch. Chicken perch. Consciousness returned with a snap; I was in Kooka Kabin.

The night before, when Lou had rushed into the Kabin and found the wonka table, he'd turned round and rushed straight out again, almost colliding with Mrs. Mulroony.

"Where—where are the other units, Mrs. Mulroony?" he whispered hoarsely. He stressed the word *units* and it sounded funny, drifting out over Mrs. Mulroony's backyard, the way *discos* had sounded in the dark street outside Mr. Finnegan's store.

He was still hoping, I thought, still painfully struggling to convince himself that there were other Kabins somewhere out there, *real* Kabins, the kind Broadside Williams had described, with fitted carpet and air-conditioning, water beds and spa baths and spotless bachelor kitchens that the bachelors never used.

"Other units, dear?" wondered Mrs. Mulroony.

"You know, apartments, holiday flats, chalets, cabanas—"

Mrs. Mulroony gave Lou a long, considering look. When she spoke to him again it was in that slow, deliberate manner I'd used on Mr. Finnegan, as if she thought Lou might have a problem with language, or possibly with his mind. "Oh, there's only the one, dear. My Alf fixed it up just before he passed away. He *was* planning to put up another one—so we'd have twinnies, you know—but then he didn't have the time, poor soul." She gave the narrow door a gentle pat and looked lovingly round the interior of the Kabin. "Used to be the old chook house, this did," she said softly. "Not that you'd know, of course. He rebuilt it from the ground up, like."

Chook house! I raised my head groggily from the pillow. "Cock-a-doodle-do!" I screeched. There was no answering crow from Lou's bed, and when I looked more closely, I saw that it was empty.

Lou wasn't what you'd call an early riser, and a sudden wave of panic seized me. Could he have gone, lit out back home? But when I thought it over, the panic subsided at once. Lou was the kind of person who always took ages to make up his mind about anything. He had this little notebook, and whenever he had to make a decision he'd write all the positive reasons on one side of the page and all the negative ones on the other. The columns always came out exactly even and then he'd get paralysed. Mostly I'd put him out of his misery by tossing a coin.

No, I couldn't see Lou leaving Scutchthorpe without all the appropriate paperwork; besides, he wouldn't go without me. And he had no place to go to, except Bilbar. I couldn't picture him figuring out all the practical stuff, like finding out when the Melbourne bus passed through Scutchthorpe. If there was a morning bus. And would it stop for him? I wondered. Thinking of that bus driver's diabolical sneer, it was easy to imagine him accelerating when he saw a customer waiting by the roadside, zooming past in a cloud of dust, with a chummy wave of his hand and a couple of toots on his antique horn. Just how easy would it actually be to get *out* of Scutchthorpe? I worried.

The door burst open and blinding sunlight filled the room. At least the weather was good, I thought. Later on we could find the beach, have a swim, take the boards out if the surf was up. Think positive! I told myself.

The sun hadn't done Lou much good, by the look of him. He was sweating all right, but his face was even paler than usual and the greenish shadows were blooming darkly in the bags beneath his eyes. "There's no—no—" He dashed himself down on his bed as if he didn't have the strength to finish the sentence. He must have been out back in the bathroom, I thought.

"No hot water?"

"No *beach*!"

No beach. Geez, I knew what he meant. I'd been to that sort of seaside myself, with the Capsellas. When the tide was in, the water came up high against a grassy cliff; when it was out, and it went out really far, you had to wade through acres and acres of brown slimy mud. Mr. Capsella liked those kind of beaches because there was no sand; he could sit on the grass and read in comfort just as if he was at home. "You mean it's a mud flat?" I asked. "Or is it that pebbly kind of beach, all stones?" (I'd been to one of those as well.)

"I mean there's no beach of any kind," said Lou bleakly. "I mean there's no *sea*." There was a long pause, in which I listened to him breathing in and out. "I walked and walked, must've been miles, and there's just no sea. There's no sign of it."

Something awful filtered up through my subconscious: images of faces staring, faces *smiling*—those guys at the terminal, the bus driver, Mr. Finnegan, even Mr. Finnegan's cat. The big golden eyes, the wide Cheshire grin of that cat, as it gazed, fascinated, at our surfboards. I pushed the images away; think positive! I told myself. Lou had always been a doom merchant, and his sense of direction was almost as bad as Mr. Capsella's. He'd simply missed the beach, gone the wrong way. "Which direction did you go?" I asked.

He waved limply towards the door. "Left. When you leave town over the Westgate Bridge and come up along the coast, the sea's always on the left, right? So I went left from the main road."

It sounded sensible; I knew I'd have taken that direction myself. Mr. Finnegan's cat leered at me again and mentally, I trod on his tail. Think positive! It occurred to me suddenly that there could be situations where thinking positive was a form of madness. But it wasn't that bad yet, I told myself firmly—perhaps, when we'd been asleep on that bus, it had taken a turn in a direction that put the coast on the right.

Reaching into my rucksack, I dragged out a pair of shorts and began pulling them on. "Let's try going right from the main road," I said.

As we crossed the dry lawn of the White House, Lou glanced towards the windows. "Let's ask Mrs. Mulroony," he suggested.

For some reason I hardly cared to examine, I didn't want to ask Mrs. Mulroony where the sea was—not just yet. "She might still be asleep," I muttered.

"It's ten o'clock!" A soft, dreamy expression replaced the tense, anxious look on Lou's face. Somehow I knew he was calculating the time in Stockholm. Why was he so hung up on Sweden? Just at the moment, it seemed the least of my worries.

"She might sleep late," I said briskly, grabbing his arm and steering him towards the road. "C'mon. If we don't get anywhere, *then* we'll ask her."

We didn't get anywhere. We walked and walked, first along a narrow sandy track that looked promising, and then when the track ended abruptly up against a wire fence, on through the paddocks of Scutchthorpe, acres and acres of long dry prickly grass, unexpected rabbit holes, cowpats, the occasional cow. Another fence, another paddock, each one bigger than the next, and not a sign of the sea. No blue line on the horizon, no sandhills, no cool, whispery breeze with the tang of salt in it.

"It's like crossing the continent with Burke and Wills," I moaned. "We should have brought a drink."

Lou collapsed suddenly on the grass, then rose again hastily, brushing something from the back of his shorts. "Let's go back," he pleaded.

"Can we try just one more paddock? The ground seems to be sloping a bit, and perhaps when we get to the top of the slope—"

"It'll slope down and then up again, like it did all the other times you said that."

"Possibly. But if—" I stopped myself just in time. Thinking positive *was* a form of madness, out here, anyway. "Okay," I agreed. "We'll go and ask Mrs. Mulroony."

■ ■ ■

Mrs. Mulroony didn't seem to feel the heat. Still clad in her hot-pink dressing gown, a pair of furry slippers on her feet, she was hanging a row of washing on the line. "Been for a bit of a stroll, boys?"

I couldn't quite muster up an answer and Lou got in first. "Mrs. Mulroony," he bleated, "is there a beach around here?"

"A beach, pet?" Mrs. Mulroony gave Lou another of those long, considering gazes, and this time there was a trace of pity in it. She patted him gently on the cheek. "There's no beach here, love. Heavens above, pet, how could there be? We're more than two hundred kilometres from the sea!"

"Oh," gulped Lou. "Thank you, Mrs. Mulroony." He backed away from her caressing hand and slouched across the grass towards the Kabin.

I was about to follow him when Mrs. Mulroony whispered, "Is *that* why he brought those surf things along? I did *wonder*. Did he think you were taking him to the seaside, dear?" She gazed after Lou's small, hunched figure and shook her head sadly. "I always think it's such a shame when they look like that."

"Look like what, Mrs. Mulroony?"

"Why, practically normal, like he does, poor thing. Why, to look at him, first off, you wouldn't think there was anything wrong with him, would you?" She gave a long, flowing sigh. "I don't suppose my talking about the beach being two hundred kilometres away made much sense to him; he wouldn't know what a kilometre was, would he?" She clucked her tongue sympathetically.

Light dawned on me suddenly. She thought we were cracked. Or at least, I realised with treacherous relief, she thought Lou was. "He's okay, Mrs. Mulroony. Honest," I assured her. "He understood every word you said; he's very intelligent. He came first in English last semester."

"It's always the clever ones you have to watch, isn't it, love? Why would he bring a surfboard—two surfboards—to a place two hundred kilometres from the sea?" She smiled at me. "It was good of you to carry the other one, dear."

"The other one's mine, Mrs. Mulroony."

"Yours?" Mrs. Mulroony backed away slightly, and her voice changed. "Is it now, dear?"

"Yes. We brought them because we're stopping off at a friend's place on the way home—*he* lives near the beach."

Her face cleared. "Oh, I *see*. You know, if you feel in need of a dip while you're here, there's O'Reilly's dam, just a couple of kilometres down the track. Mr. O'Reilly

won't mind you swimming there. I'd be careful, though—
he lost a couple of sheep a few weeks back."

"Thanks, Mrs. Mulroony."

"Just tell him Maureen sent you."

"Sure, we'll do that."

■　■　■

"She thinks I'm a nut case, doesn't she?" Lou gulped down
a tumbler of water from the tap over the sink. Its brownish
tinge—rust? sludge?—made me think suddenly of the delicate stomach that had carried Mr. Mulroony off. Death by
water.

"I told her you were okay. It was a natural mistake."

He glanced at me over the rim of the glass. "What do
you mean, a natural mistake?"

"I mean, it was just that you happened to be the one
who asked about the beach, and as we seem to be two
hundred kilometres inland, you can see how it looked like
a barmy question. Anyway, forget about it, I put her
straight, she doesn't think you're a nut case anymore."

"Doesn't she?" He narrowed his eyes. "I'll bet she
does."

"Look, let's have breakfast."

"On what?" he asked.

It was a good question. We hadn't thought to bring groceries to Scutchthorpe; we'd expected the place to be full
of fast-food joints. The most we'd have needed, so we
thought, would be orange juice, milk, and the odd packet
of cornflakes, just in case we ever chanced to get up early
for breakfast.

There was a kitchen in Kooka Kabin. Of sorts. The small
boxlike compartment was screened off from the main room

by a limp pink curtain of exactly the same shade as Mrs. Mulroony's dressing gown. Inside the box an ancient fridge, stove, and sink stood grouped together like three old soldiers commemorating World War I. Above the sink, another varnished chook perch held a motley collection of china and cutlery. We found an old plastic carrier bag under the sink and headed off for Mr. Finnegan's store.

As we approached it, Lou brightened suddenly. "Hey, do you think he sells mincemeat?" he asked excitedly. "And sour cream?"

"Dunno about the mincemeat," I replied. "But any cream he's got is bound to be sour in this heat. What do you want them for? Hamburgers?"

"No, no. Swedish meatballs. You cook them in sour cream; I thought we might be able to whack some up for dinner."

"Do you know how to make them?"

"Sure, I looked up the recipe in a Swedish cookbook. It's easy."

"You seem to know a lot about Sweden these days," I remarked casually. He didn't hear me.

Mr. Finnegan's store had come into view down the road and Lou was belting towards it. By the time I caught up, he was already through the curtain of plastic streamers that floated over the doorway and up at the counter asking for mincemeat.

Mr. Finnegan said he didn't have any on hand, but he could get some from O'Reilly, if we really wanted it.

"Is that the O'Reilly who owns the dam?" I asked.

"Yep."

"Forget it, Mr. Finnegan, I don't think we want any mincemeat."

"Hey, wait a minute," yelped Lou. "What about the Swedish meatballs?"

"What about the couple of missing sheep?" I whispered.

"Missing sheep?"

I drew him aside and gave him the gist of Mrs. Mulroony's warning about O'Reilly's dam.

"You mean he might have found the sheep and used them for mince?" he gasped.

I pulled him behind a tall display of paper towels. "Keep your voice down. He's probably a mate of O'Reilly's. The mince could be perfectly okay, but I just wouldn't like to take the chance. Funny things can happen in the country."

"Yeah." He frowned. "Didn't Mr. Mulroony pass on from some kind of stomach trouble?"

"You've got it."

"We've definitely decided, Mr. Finnegan," said Lou, fronting up to the counter again. "We don't want any mincemeat. We've changed our minds. Or any sour cream."

Mr. Finnegan shrugged. "Don't keep sour cream anyway. There's no call for it round here. We like our food fresh." He paused, and added meaningfully: "In the country."

We stocked up on cornflakes and some battered, rust-specked cans of pineapple juice, then added spaghetti and baked beans and a frozen chicken for dinner. Mr. Finnegan rang the figures up on his till—for the price of that lot, I thought, we could have eaten out in a five-star restaurant.

"I hear you two were lookin' for the beach," he chuckled.

How did he know that? I glanced nervously towards the door, half expecting to see a flash of bright pink as Mrs.

Mulroony slipped out of sight. And then I realised: even in Scutchthorpe they had telephones.

"Not exactly," I said swiftly. "Just somewhere to swim. We thought there might be a river or something."

"Just O'Reilly's dam. Watch your step, though; he lost a bullock last week."

"I thought it was a couple of sheep."

"Them too." He snorted gleefully. "There's a saying round here: 'If anything's missing, you'll find it in O'Reilly's dam.' "

"Thanks for the warning."

He grinned. "It's on the house."

Slinging the loaded carrier bag between us, we headed for the door. Halfway there, Mr. Finnegan called after us, "What youse was looking for was Scutchthorne."

We spun around. *"Scutchthorne?"*

"Yeah, it's down along the coast, couple of hundred kilometres away; went there with the family once."

"Was it—did it have—"

"Discos?" He chuckled softly. "Nope. It was a quiet family place, safe for the kiddies." He paused, patting the front of his *Aloha!* T-shirt. "I prefer somewhere a bit more lively myself, now the kids are bigger. You wouldn't catch me in a dump like Scutchthorne again, no sir. I'm off to Bali in a week—family's already there. Had to wait on till my cousin came down from Newtown to take over the store." He smiled at us slyly. "Newtown in Sydney, that is."

Lou suddenly dropped his side of the carrier bag. His eyes were bulging furiously from their sockets. "When were you at Scutchthorne, Mr. Finnegan?" he asked.

"Last summer."

"Did you happen to come across a kid there, about our

age, a fat, slobby kid who looks like he's been put together from used spare parts? He'd have been with a mate."

"Plenty of fat boys there, but not with mates. Any kids I saw were with their parents. Like I said, it's a real family place."

Lou picked up his side of the carrier bag and we began battling our way out through the plastic streamers.

"Great sweatshirts you're wearing," Mr. Finnegan called after us. "Really great." He gave a low, loathsome chuckle. "All dressed up and nowhere to go!"

"One place I'm not going," growled Lou, "is back in there. And if he says that one more time, I'm going to, I'm going to—"

"He only said it once."

"But he's going to say it again," muttered Lou. "I *know* he is."

I didn't argue with him.

■ ■ ■

We spent the afternoon sunbaking on the White House lawn. It wasn't that bad: if you closed your eyes and just concentrated on the warmth of the sun you could imagine you were on a beach somewhere, and the low whine of Mrs. Mulroony's television could even pass for the crooning of couples making out on the sand . . . if you edited out the organ music.

"How long do you think that chicken's going to take to cook?" worried Lou.

"Huh?"

"That chicken we bought for dinner."

"Oh, that. Search me."

"I am. You're the one who did home ec in year eight."

"We only did scones and scrambled eggs. You asking me how to cook a chicken because I did year-eight home ec is like me asking you to sew up that rip in my shorts because you did year-seven needlework."

Lou struggled up into a sitting position. "Ouch!" he yelled. His bare chest was a brilliant, flaring crimson, red as a stoplight at midnight. One thing was for sure: if Mr. Finnegan's frozen chickens cooked as fast as Lou, we'd have dinner on the table in no time at all.

"I think we should put the thing on now," he said, "if we want it ready in time."

"Forget it," I yawned. "Let's eat out."

"Eat out? Where?"

"There must be somewhere round here. Not in Scutchthorpe, but down the road a bit. A service station restaurant, or something like that. Let's ask Mrs. Mulroony."

Mrs. Mulroony seemed puzzled when we asked her if there was somewhere we could eat. "Haven't you found it?" she asked.

"Umm, no."

"Well, come and I'll show you." She bustled off across the lawn, beckoning us to follow.

"See, I told you," I said. "I knew there'd have to be someplace. Where would they all go on Mother's Day?"

Lou wasn't convinced. "Why is she going over to the Kabin?"

"What?" Sure enough, Mrs. Mulroony was walking straight through the door of Kooka. "Here you are, boys," she carolled, as we followed her through the pink kitchen curtains. "There's everything you need in here: fridge, stove, running water." She gave a low chuckle, the feminine version of Mr. Finnegan's, only there was no malice in it. "Trust a couple of men not to be able to find the kitchen."

"Oh thanks, Mrs. Mulroony, that's just great. But it's not exactly what we meant. We meant, is there someplace round here where we could eat *out*?"

Mrs. Mulroony gazed through the open door of the Kooka, over the paddocks of Scutchthorpe, shading her eyes against the glare. "There's a nice spot over by the Spiggotts' old place," she told us. "Few shade trees, grand view of the highway. Not all that far from O'Reilly's dam, either, if you want to take a dip after you've finished eating. Few mosquitos around at this time of the day, though, and the flies can give you a real nasty bite if you let them settle. Pity it's such a still afternoon; always better to have a picnic when the wind's up, isn't it? Keeps the insects away."

"We didn't mean a picnic, Mrs. Mulroony. We meant is there a place to eat out, *inside*?"

"Inside, love?"

"An inside *place*. You know, a restaurant or something."

"Oh, you mean a restaurant!"

"Well, one of those petrol station cafs would do. We thought there might be one up the highway."

"Oh dear, no, there's nothing like that round here, pet. Mr. Finnegan runs the petrol station, and he doesn't do eats."

"Yeah, sure, Mrs. Mulroony." I felt strangely exhausted. "We just thought—"

"Tell you what, though, there's a French restaurant up the Weeba Road."

"A French restaurant!" We goggled at her.

"Yes. It's called The Left Bank. Used to be the old Weeba Bank, but when they went bust last year someone turned the place into a restaurant. People are funny, aren't they?" she mused. "You'd think they'd have called it The Sold Bank, wouldn't you, or else something French?"

"How far is it up the Weeba Road, Mrs. Mulroony?"

"About forty kilometres, pet."

"Forty kilometres!" Lou sat down heavily into one of the old armchairs. His elbow knocked the table. "*Wonka wonka wonka,*" it said.

"On *dear,*" Mrs. Mulroony whispered to me. "He's *that* disappointed, poor soul. You can see it in his face. I don't like to see them get a disappointment, not when they're like that, do you?" She shook her head sadly. Lou had been right: it was clear she did still think he was a nut case. "I'd drive you up there myself if I wasn't waiting on a call from my girls this evening," she went on. "Bound hand and foot, I am, even though they're two thousand kilometres away, waiting on that telephone. I'd rather fancy a night out myself, get the old gladrags on and kick up my heels for once. It doesn't do you any harm to have a bit of fun now and again."

"Oh, that's all right, Mrs. Mulroony—don't worry about us, we'll be fine. We'll have dinner here. We've got a chicken we bought down at Mr. Finnegan's and it won't take us a minute to pop it in the oven."

Mrs. Mulroony beamed at me. "A chicken, eh? Nothing beats a good roast chook, does it?"

■ ■ ■

"You should have asked her how to cook it," muttered Lou. "I'd have asked her myself except she'd probably have warned me not to play with stoves. I thought you said you told her I was okay."

"I did. She couldn't have heard me."

"Oh, come off it. You mean she didn't *believe* you. She took one look and thought there was something wrong with me."

I took a pair of kitchen shears from the chook perch and began sawing at the plastic bag that contained Mr. Finnegan's chicken. "Hey, what kind of scissors are these? They hardly cut, and when they do they leave this funny little pattern, like a row of triangles."

Lou glanced up. "They're pinking shears," he said. "You use them for dressmaking." He grinned at me. "Don't you know anything?"

"Year-seven needlework finally pays dividends." I grinned back.

"Comes home to roost," chortled Lou, glancing up at the varnished perch above my head.

8

*T*hree days later. Three days of sunbaking on Mrs. Mulroony's back lawn and a single visit to O'Reilly's dam, where we found no missing livestock but plenty of leeches. Three days and three raw chooks later, I wandered down the road to ring Mrs. Capsella. We couldn't face another raw meal and no matter how long we cooked Mr. Finnegan's chickens, even if we left them in the oven till they were black outside, they were red and stringy inside. Normally I wouldn't have chosen to ask Mrs. Capsella a question about cookery, she was fairly vague about the details herself, but we were too embarrassed to ask Mrs. Mulroony; she'd have felt sorry for us. Besides, I thought grimly, I had a bone to pick with Mrs. Capsella, and it wasn't a chicken bone.

I noticed she picked up the telephone at the very first ring, as if she'd been sitting right beside it for the last three days. "I'm so glad you rang!" she cried. "I've been worried something might have happened."

"I sent you a postcard the first day we came, Mum. Didn't you get it?"

That would be just like Mr. Finnegan, I thought. He ran the post office from the back counter of his store, and when he did postal business he put on this little peaked cap and a pair of rubber sleeve-protectors, even if he was only selling you a stamp. I knew that when we disappeared through the plastic streamers he forgot all about being official. I wouldn't have put it past him to read our postcards for laughs, even white over the messages, steam off the stamps, and resell the cards. We were a source of never-ending amusement for him. Every time we came in through the streamers and every time we walked out he cried: "All dressed up and nowhere to go!" and each time we vowed we'd never go back there.

The trouble was that there was so little to do in Scutchthorpe that walking down to Finnegan's store had become a kind of treat, even the highlight of our day. We'd buy cans of soft drinks and packets of stale crisps, and wander round among the groceries reading the printing on the backs of boxes and the labels on tins. It's surprising how much information you can pick up that way. Lou had even found a tin of sardines that came from Sweden, with a picture of jolly Swedish fisherfolk on the lid. I was curious about what he'd done with that picture; I suspected he might be keeping it under his pillow. I'd never check up, of course—no one, not even a parent, would stoop so low as to look under someone's pillow.

"Oh yes, I got the postcard," Mrs. Capsella said. "It came yesterday. That's what was worrying me—why is it from Adelaide?"

"It isn't from Adelaide, Mum, it just has a picture of Adelaide on the front. There weren't any with pictures of Scutchthorpe."

"Oh. All sold out, were they?"

All sold out. In the three days we'd been there we'd only ever seen two people in town besides Mr. Finnegan and Mrs. Mulroony: an elderly guy with a box under his arm going into the store ("O'Reilly delivering the mince," Lou had hissed), and a very small old lady who lived in the cottage at the other end of town. "You must be the boys from Mrs. Mulroony's," she'd said as we passed by her front fence on one of our long time-killing walks. "The boys who brought the surfboards." She'd smiled at us kindly. "Got them for Christmas, did you? I got the sweetest little mechanical mouse for Christmas once when I was a girl—I took it with me *everywhere*. I called it Jerome. You get attached to things when you're young, don't you?"

"No, they weren't sold out, Mum," I said. "There just weren't any. There's nothing much in Scutchthorpe you could actually use for a picture postcard."

"Oh." There was a silence on the end of the line, and I wondered if it was a guilty one. Had she *known*? This was the bone I wanted to pick.

"Mum, did you know about Scutchthorpe?"

"Know about it? Know what about it?"

"Did you know it was a real dump? That there's absolutely nothing here except a bunch of bristly paddocks and a rotten old dam with leeches and dead sheep at the bottom, and a single store run by this jerk who's always saying 'All dressed up and nowhere to go,' and there's not even—there's not even any *sea*." My voice had taken on the pitiful wail of an eight-year-old who'd been given a geometry set for Christmas. I hadn't really meant to tell her all this stuff, it had just come bursting out. I suddenly remembered all that guff I'd told her about holidays on your own being a maturing experience: I seemed to have regressed. I choked the words off, glancing out through the smeary pane of the telephone box. Down the road I could see Mr. Finnegan standing outside his store; he was probably listening to every word: sounds carried a long way in Scutchthorpe, perhaps because there were so few of them.

I lowered my voice to a whisper. "Mum," I asked, "did you know there wasn't any sea at Scutchthorpe?"

"No sea?" Mrs. Capsella sounded genuinely surprised. "I don't understand. You boys took those surfboards; why on earth would you do that if you weren't going to the sea?"

I drew in a long, long breath. "Mum, that guy at the Tourist Bureau, Mr. Pinkle—did he happen to mention a place called Scutchthorne to you, by any chance?"

"Scutchthorne?" There was a small silence. "Yes, he did, now you come to mention it."

"What did he say?"

"Nothing, really. Just, when I started to make the booking for Scutchthorpe, he asked me if I meant Scutchthorne. He seemed surprised I'd want to book a holiday in Scutchthorpe, but I thought that was because, well, because it was a rowdy, noisy, violent sort of place and I didn't look the type to go there." She added happily, "You mean it's not like that?"

"I just told you what it's like, Mum. It's one of those tiny little places you pass on the road to somewhere else and you wonder how anyone can live there, or what they'd do with themselves if they did."

"Oh dear." There was another silence, a long one this time. "You know," she said at last, "he *did* say something like that, but I thought he was joking."

"What did he say?"

"He said, 'I think you might find it rather quiet there.' But you see, he had this nasty little smile on his face and I thought he was being sarcastic; that what he really meant—he seemed to think *I* was taking the holiday—was that I'd never be able to sleep because of the noise of motorbikes and rock music and people screaming all night—I expect he thought I was too old for that kind of thing. So I just made the booking for two and walked out."

I couldn't think of a thing to say. Mrs. Capsella went on: "You mean there's nothing like that there? No motorbikes, no souped-up rusty cars, no drunken drivers, no discos?"

"I told you, Mum, there's nothing, absolutely nothing. A three-year-old would be safer at Scutchthorpe than he'd be at home in his own cot. Even if he was taking a holiday on his own."

"Oh." She gave an enormous sigh of relief. Now she could get a good night's rest, I thought bitterly. There's something about being a parent that seems to sap the humanity right out of a person.

"But why on earth did you two want to go to a place like that?" she asked. "It sounds terribly boring."

"Because there was a mistake, Mum," I said icily. "It seems we should have gone to Scutchthorne."

"Oh dear, what a pity! You know, I *did* ask you if you were quite sure it was Scutchthorpe. But you said it was and you sounded so sure of it, and I didn't want to interfere. You might have thought I was trying to put you off or something." She paused. "Would you like to come home? Your father and I could drive up tomorrow—"

"No! No, don't do that," I said quickly.

Scutchthorpe was deadly, but we couldn't afford to go back home early. If any of the kids at school found out, we'd never live it down. "Don't tell anyone about all this, will you?" I said. "Don't tell any of our friends, or any of their mothers, that Lou and I ended up in a dump. Okay?"

"Of course I won't. As if I'd advertise your misfortune round the neighbourhood," cried Mrs. Capsella righteously. "Besides, everyone's away."

"Just don't *ever* tell them, even if they come back early." I gathered up the shreds of my self-respect. "Anyway, it's not *that* bad. What I really rang up for was—"

"Was what?"

"Do you know how to cook a frozen chicken?"

"Goodness, do you have to *cook*? Don't bother about cooking, Al, just go out somewhere. There's nothing worse than a holiday ruined by having to cook meals all the time."

I swallowed. "Mum, there's nowhere here you can eat out. If we don't cook, we don't eat."

"Oh well, it's quite simple, really. You just put the chicken in the oven for a couple of hours, at 180 degrees. No, wait, is it an old stove?"

"Yes."

"Then it'll be 350 degrees. Two hours at 350 degrees, that should do it."

"But that's what we do, and it's always sort of raw."

"Do you thaw it out first?"

"Yes," I said. "And we take the plastic bag off, too. We're not idiots, Mum."

"Of course. I keep forgetting you did that home-science course. The only thing I can think of, then, is that your chicken must be a boiler."

"What's a boiler?"

"It's a chicken, generally a pretty old chicken, that you have to boil. You just drop it in a pot of boiling water and leave it. I don't know how long it takes, probably hours, but you don't have to stand and watch it." She paused. "I don't think they taste very nice; I didn't even know people sold boilers anymore. Or ate them."

"They do in Scutchthorpe, Mum. Thanks anyway. Seeya on Saturday."

"Wait a minute, Al. Are you absolutely sure you don't want us to come and get you?"

"We'll be fine. No worries. Seeya."

"Listen—Al?"

"Yeah?"

"Don't put that chicken on overnight. Don't start boiling it in the evening and then go off to sleep; it could boil dry and start a fire, you could both be burned in your beds. And—and is the stove gas, by any chance?"

"No, it's not gas, Mum. It's perfectly safe. The whole of Scutchthorpe is safe. I told you, a toddler could manage on his own."

"He might drown in the dam."

"We don't go there, Mum. Too many leeches. Seeya."

■　■　■

As I crossed the White House lawn Lou was just coming out of Mrs. Mulroony's back door. When he saw me, he looked embarrassed. "She asked me in to watch a spot of TV," he explained. "I didn't like to say no."

"What'd you watch?"

"Public Hospital."

"Geez! I watched that once when I was home sick; it was so depressing it made me feel I should be in the hospital myself—a mental hospital."

"Yeah, that organ music's pretty lowering. But you've got to admit—" His face took on the vague, dreamy expression again.

"What do you have to admit?"

"Admit?" He stared at me, flushing slightly.

"Wake up! You said there was something you had to admit about *Public Hospital*. What was it?"

"Oh, *yes*! *Public Hospital*. You've got to admit that kind of program touches"—he gave a small cough—"universal feelings. Like, like—"

"Like love," I suggested shyly.

"Well, yes, now you mention it. There's this doctor who's been in love for forty whole years with this girl he went to school with—Betsy Jean Gilpin. She married someone else while he was at the war, and then he married someone else. It was a hopeless situation, you see, so he thought he might as well marry Rose Violet and then her husband died, but he couldn't—"

"You mean they had all that in one episode? It must have been a really tight script."

"Mrs. Mulroony filled me in on all the details. She's been watching since 1976. Her girls watch too when they're at home. She's taping all the episodes for them in case it's not on up north. Oh, and by the way, Mrs. Mulroony doesn't think I'm off the planet anymore; she saw I could follow the whole plot just like a normal person. Besides, I agreed with her that Sister Herlihy dressed far too young for her age."

Geez, I thought. A few more days watching soap operas and he'd have a real case of brain damage. "Listen," I said, dragging him back to the real world. "Mum asked if we wanted to go home early."

His eyes flashed with hope. "Did you say yes? You did, didn't you?"

"No, I didn't."

"What? Are you crazy? Four more days in this place and we'll—"

"Just listen for a minute, will you? I told her no because we'd look a real pair of idiots making such a big deal out of this holiday and then coming back early. Your dad would be really laughing up his sleeve, for a start. And you'd have to go to Bilbar."

"I could stay at your place."

"Sure you could, but it isn't just our parents. What about the other kids?"

"Geez, I forgot about them."

I frowned. "You know, it's funny we should have made a mistake like that. I'm almost sure Broadside said Scutchthorpe. Do you think he could have actually come *here*?"

"I wondered about that," said Lou. "I even asked Mrs. Mulroony; I described him exactly, but she said she'd never come across anyone who looked like that, anywhere. Besides, there hasn't been anyone in Kooka Kabin for three years. No, we got it wrong." He paused and added gloomily, "It was Fate. Let's face it, we're the kind of kids who go to Scutchthorpe."

"Scutchthorne doesn't sound any better," I said. "Except for the sea. You know what Mr. Finnegan said about it being a quiet family place. And I bet Broadside didn't go there with a mate, like he said. I bet his parents dragged him there to build sandcastles and he made up that whole story."

"Mr. Finnegan didn't see him."

"They might have gone at different times. Besides," I added, "if he went with his folks, he probably looked different."

"What do you mean?"

"Think about it. Kids look different when you see them with their parents, don't they? Smaller, younger, kind of shrunken."

"Yeah. But what are we going to *tell* people when we get back?"

"No worries. Same as Broadside did, of course."

"But what if any of them ever *come* here? Like we did? And find out."

"Then they'll keep quiet too, won't they? It's kind of like a chain letter. Everyone expects a miracle, everyone gets disappointed, and everyone keeps quiet."

"Hey, yeah! And the myth of Scutchthorpe keeps rolling on, year after year after year. Just think, in twenty years' time there might still be kids from Lawson High going on holiday to Scutchthorpe."

"Yeah." I grinned. "A real Lawson High tradition, as Irma Doone would say." *With shawms, and with cymbals, and harps of gold*, I added to myself.

9

*L*ou was a great reader, and at times I couldn't help thinking that it wasn't good for his nerves. Look at "The Celestial Omnibus"—if he'd given that story a miss like I'd done, he wouldn't have freaked out in the Yarrabung bus and begun thinking we were en route to heaven. The whole business had started way back when he was in kindergarten and his aunt Annie had given him this picture book she'd picked up in an antique shop. He'd been so shaken up when he opened it that he'd run right down to my place to show the book to me.

It was weird stuff all right: this tiny little kid had fallen through a hole in his mother's sofa and found out just what was going on down there beneath the cushions. He'd been chased through the springs and stuffing by a giant needle, an overweight cotton reel, and a sharp, long-legged pair of scissors, and when he finally found his way out again, his mother hadn't even noticed he was missing. Lou was so shaken I'd lifted up the cushions on our sofa—there was a hole there, all right, and even a needle and a cotton reel, but I'd pointed out how small they were, and how they didn't move and run about like the ones in the book.

He'd seemed okay after that, but I couldn't help noticing that he was a bit funny about sofas even now—if he walked into a living room and there was the usual setup of a sofa and a few chairs, he'd always avoid the sofa and sit on one of the chairs, even if it was the hard wooden kitchen sort.

Still, that was just Lou, I guess; he'd probably have been like that even if his aunt Annie had never given him the book, just like he might have thought the Yarrabung bus was celestial without reading the story. And it probably comforted him to find that the people who wrote the stuff he read thought in the same weird way he did.

I wasn't a great reader myself. I never seemed to get round to it. All through high school, English teachers had been adding a postscript to my report cards: "Would improve if he read more," as if I was some sort of cake with a missing ingredient. If there was one thing I hated it was people telling me I should read, just like they'd tell a little kid he should eat all his broccoli because it was good for him. When that little kid was a paunchy, balding guy of forty-five, I thought, he'd embarrass his wife and kids in restaurants, telling the waitress to take the fried rice back to the kitchen because he'd found some broccoli in it.

One of the worst aspects of my own family holidays was that Mrs. Capsella took the opportunity to bring along a large supply of books, which she left lying around in conspicuous places: on tabletops and chests of drawers, perched on the arms of sofas and even the rim of the bath where the soap container should have been. They weren't intended for her own benefit; they were aimed at me, and I mean *aimed*. She never actually *said* anything to me about reading, that wasn't her style; she simply left the books lying about and hoped I'd get so bored I'd finally be driven to read one. Or to put it another way, which was the way I'd come to feel: that I'd give in.

There wasn't a single place in those holiday shacks where you could sit, stand, or slouch without seeing the edge of a book lying in wait. It gave you a hunted feeling. And the simple, harmless truth was that I just wasn't a reading kind of person. Just as Mrs. Capsella wasn't a sporting kind of person. She might think I needed a little mental exercise, but she was equally in need of the physical kind. How would she like it, I wondered, if I took to leaving sports equipment all over the house, in every corner where it might catch her eye: an exercise bike in the middle of the bathroom, a pair of ladies' running shoes on the arm of the sofa, a tennis racquet on her bedside table? Would she suddenly feel impelled to use them? Would she pick up the runners, like she thought I'd do with the books, murmur to herself, "These look interesting," put them on, and go out for a jog? Of course she wouldn't! She'd simply avert her eyes, pretend she didn't see them. She'd feel hunted, just as I did.

She never realised this, of course. It was pitiful to watch how every single holiday she'd lay the books out in all the usual places, hoping that one dismal, boring, endless rainy day, miles from anywhere, isolated from my companions and any form of real life, I'd pick up a book and the miracle would happen: I'd be transformed into a Reader.

And suddenly, at Scutchthorpe, the miracle happened. On our fourth evening there I'd have given anything to get my hands on a book. I'd been lying on my bed for forty-five minutes counting the boats and dancing sailors on the wallpaper. There were seven hundred fifty boats and eight hundred twenty-seven sailors. Lou had drawn a chair up to the table, silenced the wonky leg with a rolled-up sweatshirt beneath it, and was busily scribbling in the notebook he used for recording his worries and the pros and cons of possible future decisions. It was the kind of activity that could keep him happily occupied for hours.

"Hey!"

He looked up at me blearily.

"Did you bring any books I could borrow?"

"Nope."

"You *didn't*? How come? You never go anywhere without a couple of books."

"I know." He gazed at me earnestly. "But this time I made a vow: I decided that while I was at Scutchthorpe I'd try to be a real guy, the sort of guy who doesn't read, like most guys are. So I left them at home. Besides," he added breezily, "I didn't think I'd have any time to read. I thought we'd be out all the time."

"Great!" I went back to counting sailors. Perhaps I'd get a different total the second time, and then I could count them again, to see which was right. By then it might be time to go to sleep.

"There's this," said Lou suddenly, reaching under the table and pulling out what looked like an old newspaper.

"What is it?"

"The *Country Times*. I found it in the laundry this morning."

"Gee, thanks." I grabbed at it eagerly and in twenty minutes I'd read the whole thing through. I was just starting the article on alpaca breeding for the second time when I glanced across the room and saw that Lou was now lying sprawled on his bed, a sheet of paper spread on the pillow, and beside it, a book!

"Hey! You've got a book! You said you didn't bring any."

"Oh, it's not a book, exactly," replied Lou carelessly.

"Not a novel or anything, it's just a—a sort of text-book."

"A textbook! You mean you're actually studying! We go off on holidays and you study?"

"I'm not studying, not schoolwork anyway." He held the book up. "It's a handbook on graphology—you know, handwriting analysis."

"You're teaching yourself how to analyse handwriting?"

"Okay, okay, no need to look at me like that. I know what you're thinking—that sort of stuff is a load of bull-shit." He smiled rather patronisingly. "I used to think like that myself."

"It's the sort of stuff the characters in *Public Hospital* would get into," I remarked.

"Hey! You're right!'" he exclaimed. "Dr. Slicer has this son who's a bit of a problem. He was a perfectly normal kind of kid until he hit fourteen and then he started creeping out of the house at midnight and not coming back till just on dawn—"

"Come off it! That's a problem? How many kids do you know who don't creep out of the house at night? Including us?" I felt a sudden sharp pang of longing; if only we could creep out the narrow door of Kooka Kabin and not come back till dawn. The problem was, I thought disgust-edly, that though the watchdogs were hundreds of kilome-tres away and we had no need to creep, there was nowhere for us to creep *to*, unless you wanted to spend the night listening to owls hoot in the paddocks.

"But we go out for special reasons," continued Lou. "When there's a party or something."

"So what does Dr. Slicer's son do?"

"That's what Dr. Slicer doesn't know. And it's got him

really worried because there's this streak of lunacy in his family that he's been keeping secret from his wife. It goes back five generations. He can't confide in his colleagues, naturally, in case they think he's got it too, so he tears a page out of the kid's schoolbook and sends it off to his graphologist in California."

"Don't tell me, let me guess! The guy writes back and says it's the definite scrawl of a werewolf."

"Dr. Slicer hasn't got the reply yet. It might come in Friday's episode. Anyway"—he leaned forward on the edge of the bed, the graphology book open on his knees—"I've been checking out a couple of examples, a few things I found at home. Dad's handwriting, for instance. He's got this really thick, heavy writing and it's almost exactly the same as the example here on page eighty-seven." He flicked over a few pages. "You know what it says?"

"What?"

His lips curled with triumph as he began to read: " 'Indicates an obstinate and aggressive character. Will get his own way by brute force and will not allow any obstacle to obstruct his path.' See? That's just like Dad, isn't it? You'd almost think the guy had met him. I'll bet he's crouched over the Monopoly board this very moment, being obstinate and aggressive. And remember how he sawed off the legs of that table? He was going at the thing like a maniac—that table was an obstacle in his path!" He slammed the book shut and wagged his head at me. "I think there's really something in it."

I wasn't convinced, and the enthusiastic expression on his face made me feel uneasy. Next thing he'd be wearing a crystal strapped to his forehead, and with that dead white skin he'd look like a two-legged unicorn. There was something *behind* it, I thought, and it wasn't just the brain softening caused by the hours he spent in front of Mrs. Mulroony's television. I was almost sure it was something to do with his interest in Sweden, and that dazed, dreamy expression he got on his face when he asked me the time.

"Anne-Marie's a problem, though," he said suddenly. I looked up to see him squinting down at the piece of paper on his pillow. "Her writing's just like printing," he went on, "and I can't find a single example in the book that fits it—they don't say a word about people who print."

"Who's Anne-Marie?"

"Anne-Marie?" His head jerked up and he flushed a sticky shade of crimson, like a raspberry icy pole.

"Yeah. Anne-Marie. You were just talking about her printing."

"Oh, *that* Anne-Marie," he mumbled. "Er, she's a girl I know, a girlfriend, I mean, a friend who's a girl."

"Is she Swedish?"

He stared at me in astonishment, his mouth wide open, as if I'd just displayed amazing powers of extrasensory perception. "How'd you know that?"

"I didn't know, I just guessed. You seem so interested in Sweden all of a sudden."

"It's not 'all of a sudden,'" he said defensively. "I've always been interested in Sweden, and since I met Anne-Marie, well naturally—"

"Naturally. How'd you get hold of her?"

"What?" His pale eyes widened with horror.

"Sorry, I meant, how did you get to know her?"

"Oh." He tugged shyly at the end of his sweatshirt, pulling it down over his red, roasted ribs. "She's the daughter of one of Dad's friends, this guy he met at a conference."

"Really? What's she like? Is she tall and blonde?" I hesitated—was I being a racist? But Lou made no objection, so I went on. "Does she go to private school?" I figured she must do; there were definitely no Swedish girls at Lawson High, tall and blonde or otherwise.

"Oh, um—I haven't actually met her, not like that."

I stared at him. "How do you mean, 'not like that'?"

"Well, she wasn't here with her dad. He was just visiting, and she couldn't come because it was the school term in Sweden. We're—" he gave another shy little tug to his sweatshirt—"just writing to each other. See, her father told Dad she was looking for a penfriend in Australia. And so I wrote, and she replied." He picked up the sheet of paper from his pillow and held it out to me. "This is her *fifth* letter. See what I mean about the writing? You can't really analyse printing—"

I glanced at the rounded, even letters; it was a bit like the sort of writing you did back in infant school, before you got into grade two and started joining up letters. Cherry Clagg still used that style. Because the print was so clear and the sentences so short I couldn't help reading a couple of them, though I didn't mean to. "I am going to be a fir tree in the School Pageant," I read, and lower down, beneath a row of kisses, there was a P.S.: "I am teaching Gustave to fetch in Daddy's newspaper."

"Did she send you a photograph?" I asked.

Lou snatched the letter away. "You know, you're completely hung up on people's physical appearance. It's sexist."

"No, I'm not. I was just curious; it's natural when you hear about someone and don't know what they look like. Anyway," I went on, "you can tell a lot more about people from their photographs than you can from their handwriting. Remember the photograph Mrs. Slewt showed us that time, the one her dad took of her with the kittens? She was ten years old and she already had that look on her face she gets when she's handing out exam papers. Pure sadism. And the way she was holding the kitten by the ear, it's just the way she used to get hold of Broadside Williams when she was shoving him out of class. Not that I think Anne-Marie's photo would show anything like that," I added hastily.

"It doesn't."

"You've got one, have you? Give us a look. Or don't you want to? I'll understand if it's private."

"Okay, okay." He grinned, reaching under his pillow. I could see he was really dying to show me. As he drew it out, I caught a glimpse of the picture from the sardine tin. I wondered what other Swedish mementoes he might be keeping there and felt relieved we'd never risked O'Reilly's mince and made the meatballs.

The photo wasn't quite what I'd expected. It showed a chubby baby girl in a frilly dress sitting plumb in the middle of an enormous furry rug. I stared at it for some time; there's not much you can tell from a baby's face in the way of character. She was smiling, though.

"Looks like she's got a real sense of humour," I remarked feebly.

"That's what I thought!" cried Lou happily. He craned forward. "See what she's written on the back?"

I flipped it over. "This photograph is a few years old," I read, in that same careful, even printing.

"Uh, a real sense of humour," I repeated.

I handed the photograph back and Lou replaced it ten-

· 104 ·

derly beneath the pillow. Then he flopped down on the bed, his arms behind his head, gazing dreamily at the ceiling. I thought the conversation had ended, but just as I picked up the *Country Times* again he asked, "What kind of costume do you suppose she'd wear to play a fir tree?"

An image from the distant past floated into my head: Melissa Pole and Emma Chipper and Irma Doone singing "Trees" at the grade-one concert. They wore brown cardboard tubes pasted over with cutout leaves, and streamers of green crepe paper fluttered from their shoulders and the tops of their heads. "Uh, something soft and green and floating," I replied.

There was something wrong here, I thought. Surely no teenager worth her salt would stand up in front of the whole school dressed in a cardboard tube. Only little kids could be forced to appear in public in that kind of getup. Even at age seven Melissa and the others had made a fuss. Emma had told Miss Fanshawe the costume made them look like three giant toilet rolls, and Melissa had complained that when she came to the line "and lift her leafy arms to pray" she couldn't do the actions because she couldn't get her arms out of the tube. As for Irma Doone, she'd burst into tears and rushed off the stage, crying that they were making the poem look silly.

"Green and floating," murmured Lou. "That's exactly what I imagined." He was silent for a moment, then he said, "She must be pretty tall to play a fir tree."

"Guess so. She looks like a pretty big baby."

He turned towards me, resting his head on one hand. "I've been thinking of asking her how tall she is every time I write, but I always put it off—I'm a bit nervous I'll find out she's taller than me." He added gloomily: "A lot taller."

"You've got a few more years to grow," I said, sounding like someone's mother. "Anything could happen."

"Yeah." He gulped. "That's what's bothering me."

"What's a few feet between friends?" I grinned. "If you've finished with that graphology book, could I have it? I need something else to read."

"Okay. Chuck us the *Country Times*, willya?"

I tossed it over. "There's a good article on alpaca breeding on page seventeen," I told him.

Half an hour later, after carefully analysing my own signature, I learned that I had a placid disposition and was inclined to violence. I was also secretive and deceitful and had an honest, open nature. And there was the possibility that I had criminal tendencies. So much for the science of graphology, I thought, at least in my case.

Lou had finished the *Country Times* and was staring up at the ceiling again. "Want me to switch off the light?" I asked.

He sighed. "May as well. What time is it?" He asked the question so many times I was in danger of getting repetitive sprain injury.

"Ten o'clock." Ten o'clock! I hadn't been to bed that early since primary school. All the same, I didn't even hear Lou telling me what time it was in Stockholm; I went out like a light. There's something about doing nothing all day that wears you out.

10

■

*T*here's all that grey foamy stuff again," observed Lou disgustedly, peering down into the big pot where Mr. Finnegan's boiler was, well, boiling.

It happened every time, and it made you wonder whether the chook was really a chook at all, or something that O'Reilly might have shot down in the bristly paddocks round his dam—a giant magpie or maybe even a crow.

When we scooped the chook out of the pot it was always crusted over with a layer of the scummy foam, the sort of stuff you saw cruising down stormwater drains after a heavy downpour. It was hard to scrape off. You could wash it off all right, the problem being that there was only a cold-water tap in the Kooka kitchen and when you'd washed the foam away the chicken was stone cold and more unappetising than ever. There was a hot-water tap outside in the laundry shed, but somehow we didn't feel good about washing our dinner in a laundry tub. Besides, it was cold again by the time we got it back inside.

This time we gave the chicken a brisk rubdown with the tea towel and it was still sort of warm when we finally got it onto our plates.

"Tastes foul, doesn't it," gagged Lou, struggling to down his first mouthful.

"I wish it did—taste like fowl, I mean. The funny thing

is how when it's cooked it doesn't have any taste at all. It didn't taste of anything when it was raw, either, but we were so bust trying to chew it we didn't notice."

Lou waved his fork. "Have you ever thought how it's kind of eerie?"

"What is?"

"That we should be cooking chooks in a chook house. It's like cannibals eating their meal in the victim's living room." He glanced uneasily toward the varnished chook perches up on the wall, as if he half-expected to hear a ghostly cackle of protest.

"Anything that has the hide to taste like this deserves to be eaten," I said callously.

"Here." Lou pushed the sauce bottle across the table. "Makes it taste better, makes it taste of something, anyway, even if it's only tomato sauce."

I shook the bottle. We'd only bought it that afternoon, but Mr. Finnegan's tomato sauce had a habit of clogging right from the start.

Splat!

"Geez!" The exclamation came from both of us. Half the contents of the bottle had splattered onto the front of my sweatshirt.

"It's your best Gag sweatshirt!" gasped Lou. "And—and it's white!"

"*Was* white, you mean." I felt like crying. I'd never get that stain out, the shirt was ruined, and it had cost me three solid weekends of hard labour, mowing lawns round the neighbourhood.

"Quick! Quick!" bawled Lou. "Don't just sit there, it'll *set*. Get it off; you have to do something fast."

"Like what?" I pulled the sweatshirt over my head.

"Put it in something. Stain remover. Oh—" He clapped his hand to the side of his head. "I forgot, there isn't any."

Mr. Finnegan didn't sell stain remover. When Lou had got melted tar from the highway all over the bottoms of his new jeans, Mr. Finnegan had only been able to offer paint stripper.

"Cold water," I sighed. "Water's all we've got, anyway."

"Yeah!" Lou grabbed the shirt from my hands and was about to dump it into the sink, right on top of all the grey chicken scum, when I grabbed it back. "Not in there! The laundry!"

We dashed out the back and across the lawn. The laundry was housed in a lean-to shed against the back fence, and it was what you might call primitive. There was no washing machine, just two stone tubs beside the old bath we used for our morning wash.

Laundry was a major problem at Kooka Kabin. It used up a lot of our time, which in one sense was a good thing, as we had so much of it on our hands. White was the fashionable colour that summer, and though we'd brought enough gear to last us a week in a resort, we needed even more at Scutchthorpe. You had to change three times a day, not because you were going places, but for simple everyday reasons like dust and dirt and cookery stains. When we'd washed our stuff in the tubs we had to wring it out by hand, an exhausting job that made you feel like the Boston Strangler.

Then we'd cart it across to Mrs. Mulroony's clothesline. Drying was no problem because of the heat, but our clothes dried stiff as cardboard and worried painfully at Lou's sunburn. A dose of fabric softener would have helped, but Mr. Finnegan probably didn't stock that either, and if we'd asked him for some, the news would have been all over town five minutes after we left the store.

The sweatshirt floated in the tub, the stain darkening ominously. "There's something you use for tomato sauce stains," said Lou vaguely. "I can't remember what it is." He looked at me hopefully. "You could ring up your mum and ask." I knew how his mind worked. He was hoping she'd ask if we wanted to come back home, or even that the sound of my voice on the telephone again might prompt her to come and get us. He was in danger of losing his self-respect. "She wouldn't know," I said, remembering the tennis ball.

"Mrs. Mulroony might, but it's embarrassing asking her for household hints all the time. Hey, I know! They keep books in libraries about that sort of thing; they're in the domestic-science section."

"There's no library in Scutchthorpe," I reminded him.

"Geez, yeah! I forgot where we were for a moment. Hey, what about women's magazines?"

"Women's magazines?"

"They have letters on that kind of thing, even contests. All these ladies write in with tips on how to get out different types of stains and the best one wins five dollars. And then they publish the whole lot. Mr. Finnegan sells women's magazines."

It was an idea, and it also gave us something to do the next morning, something besides sunbaking and taking walks along the back roads, hoping, like toddlers, to see a kangaroo. It was almost something to look forward to, so you could wake up and feel the day had some kind of a purpose. When we opened our eyes next morning we could hardly wait till nine o'clock, when Mr. Finnegan opened his doors for business.

■ ■ ■

"All dressed up and nowhere to go!"

It didn't have the same effect it once had; familiarity had toughened us up, and Mr. Finnegan could simply have been saying, "Nice day outside." He said that too, a moment later.

"Great," we replied.

"Surf's up," he chortled.

We ignored him, sneaking round the grocery stacks to the distant corner where he kept his women's magazines. It was a well-placed location, hidden from the counter by the towering pyramid of paper towels. Faintly, his voice floated over to us. "Anything I can do for you?"

"No thanks, Mr. Finnegan. We're just looking."

We crouched down behind the paper towels, snatched up a couple of magazines, and began browsing. Some time later, halfway through "Ask Dr. Kate," I remembered the purpose of our visit and hissed at Lou: "You found any tomato-sauce-stain tips yet?"

"Uh, no." He flicked over a few pages. "I've been looking and looking, but I can't find a single word about tomato sauce. It's probably so basic they don't think anyone needs to know." He rubbed his eyes. "Geez, it's dark in here, isn't it? You can hardly see to read the print."

I'd been noticing this myself. Reading the last letter to Dr. Kate had been distinctly heavy going—there seemed to be a thick shadow hanging over the page. It even had a shape, rounded and headlike, and as I read on, the shadow grew longer at the bottom, as if it was sprouting a neck. I turned and found Mr. Finnegan looming over my shoulder.

"You boys planning to buy those magazines?"

We didn't know what to say. Was he asking the question,

in that rather menacing tone of voice, because boys in Scutchthorpe didn't read women's magazines? Did he think it was a greasy habit of city perverts? Or did he sound threatening because we were sitting there reading his magazines for free, entertaining ourselves at his expense? I glanced at my watch. Nine forty-five (twelve forty-five in Stockholm)—we'd been browsing for three-quarters of an hour.

Mr. Finnegan solved the problem for us by putting his hand out. "That'll be three dollars sixty," he said. "Anything else I can do for you today?"

"No thanks, Mr. Finnegan." We scrambled to our feet.

"How about another chook? Know what? Got a call from the wife last night, they had spiced steak with grated coconut for dinner. Ever had that?"

"No, Mr. Finnegan."

He smiled. "How about another chook, then?"

"I think we'll leave it, Mr. Finnegan. We're having tinned spaghetti tonight. Just give us two cans of lemonade, as usual."

"You boys drink too much of that stuff, you know," Mr. Finnegan said wisely. "It's not good for you, all those additives. Know what? You should try making up a batch of the real stuff; there's nothing to it and it's real coolin'. The wife makes it all the time when she's home." He rested his elbows comfortably on the counter. "All you need is a couple of pounds of sugar and a bunch of lemons. Mrs. Mulroony's got a lemon tree in the front yard—or there's one over at the back of O'Reilly's dam, if you're going that way today."

"Thanks, Mr. Finnegan, but I think—"

"Recipe's simple as pie, any fool could make it; you just

slice up the lemons, pour the sugar over, and then pour the water on top of that."

"Thanks, Mr. Finnegan."

He beamed at us. "Thought you'd get a kick out of it, seeing as you're interested in recipes and all that sort of stuff."

"What?"

He shot a meaningful glance towards our magazines.

"Oh. Oh, *those*. We're just using them for a school project on—on popular reading tastes."

"You don't say?"

Lou hadn't been listening to the lemonade conversation; he'd been staring through the window at the sunlit street outside with an increasingly hopeless expression on his face. Boredom. He swung round suddenly. "Mr. Finnegan," he cried. "Is there anything—anything at all—going on round here?"

Mr. Finnegan started as violently as if Lou had drawn a gun on him. "What do you mean?" he asked nervously. "What do you mean by 'anything going on'? I'm a respectable man, I'll have you know."

"No worries, Mr. Finnegan," I said quickly. "Lou didn't mean anything like that. He just meant to ask if there was anything *on* in the district, in the way of entertainment. You know, anything we could go to. Like a—like a school fete, for instance."

"A school fete?" His voice was squeaky with surprise and I didn't blame him; I simply hadn't been able to think of any form of entertainment that would be familiar to Scutchthorpe.

"School fete?" Mr. Finnegan squeaked again. "The nearest school's at Uloola and anyway, it's closed for the holidays. How could they be having a fete in the holidays? No one would go to it even if they did. Everyone's away." He peered at me suspiciously. "You two feeling all right? You haven't been takin' the water out at O'Reilly's dam, have you? You gotta be careful about that; always keep your head out of the water when you're taking a dip. That's what done Alf Mulroony in—couldn't figure how to swim with his head up."

"We're okay, Mr. Finnegan. I just forgot it was the school holidays."

"Forgot it was the school holidays!" Mr. Finnegan gasped. "How could you forget it was school holidays when you're bloody well havin' 'em?"

Good question, I thought grimly. "Yeah, well—"

"A bush dance," said Lou brightly. "That's the sort of thing we meant, Mr. Finnegan."

"Bush dance, eh?" Mr. Finnegan relaxed. "Wrong time o' year for bush dances; they're mostly in the winter. Nothing much doing round here in the summer." He tapped his fingers thoughtfully on the countertop. "Wait a minute, though—there's a 50-50 dance over at the Church Hall in Weeba. It's not all that far and Mrs. Mulroony would give you a lift."

"When is it?" The pathetic eagerness in our voices should have melted a heart of stone, but Mr. Finnegan gave a low, beastly chuckle. "April the first," he cackled. "Guess you'll be gone by then, eh? Unless you're planning to come back round Easter. Think you might?"

Stiffly, I told him we had no such plans.

We dodged out through the plastic streamers and took the long way home. Halfway along the track there was a big shady gum tree and we settled down beneath it, opened our cans, and became absorbed in the magazines again. It was a glorious day, the cicadas singing in the branches above our heads and the air as bright as gold dust. It suddenly occurred to me that this was the only holiday I'd ever taken where it hadn't rained at all. It was enough to make you weep.

Lou nudged me sharply. "Look at this," he said, pointing to a letter on the Problem Page. "It's from Speechless, of Warawee North. She'd got this problem; she's so shy she can't think of anything to say to people. They all think she's a snob and she hasn't got any friends."

"She should come to Scutchthorpe; it wouldn't matter here."

"Be serious, will you? I was thinking—" He flushed slightly.

"What were you thinking?"

"I could write to her. We could have a correspondence; she mightn't be shy on paper, and it might cure her. Do you think if I wrote to the magazine they'd give me her proper name and address?"

"Nope."

"Why not?"

"They'd think you were some kind of loony, like those funny guys who hang round outside the fence at netball practice."

"I could tell them my age."

"Wouldn't help. They'd still think you were funny."

"But this girl's just shy; writing to me might help her get over it."

"Wouldn't that be a bit unfair on Anne-Marie?" I asked slyly. "She probably thinks she's your only penfriend. If you start writing to Speechless as well, it's almost like you're two-timing her."

"As if I'd do that!" He stared at me indignantly. "Anne-

Marie's the only girl I ever met, er, came across, who's really on my wavelength." He snapped the magazine shut and gazed mistily over the paddocks. After a few seconds the misty expression cleared and he began to giggle.

"What's up?"

"Hey—hey, I just *thought* of something. If Finnegan ate some of O'Reilly's mince, by mistake, and he kicked the bucket and they had a funeral in the town, it would be, it would be—" He doubled up, clutching at his sides. "It would be *Finnegan's Wake!*"

"Finnegan's wake?" I echoed blankly.

The grin faded from Lou's face. "You don't get it, do you?" he said sadly.

"Is it a Book Joke?"

"Never mind," he sighed.

Being a reader made him lonely, I thought. He was always telling jokes like this; jokes about book titles and book characters, and none of us ever got the point, we just looked blank; he could have been speaking in Swahili. I promised myself that when we got back to town I'd look up *Finnegan's Wake* in the library; I might even read a bit of it, if I had the time. You never know, it might be an interesting yarn.

Lou was gazing out over the paddocks again. "What's the time?" he asked.

"Very early," I told him. "Very early in the morning of a long hot day in Scutchthorpe." I got to my feet. "Let's go and check out Mrs. Mulroony's lemon tree. Perhaps we could make that lemonade after all."

11

$\mathcal{E}$vening again: we lay on our beds, still browsing through the magazines.

"Hey, did you see this quiz?" asked Lou. " 'Is Your Boy-friend a Hopeless Case?' "

"Yeah," I muttered. I'd not only seen it, I'd done it, and got the second-lowest score. "This is the sort of guy you can bully—if you want to," it had said. I'd never thought of myself in that light before and I still didn't, but I couldn't deny that my score had made me uneasy. Practically every girl at school read that magazine, and they all did the quizzes.

You saw them gathered round the boiler at recess on Wednesday mornings, filling in the answers and giggling when any of us walked by. Now I knew why they giggled; reading these magazines had given me a distinct sense of being under surveillance. Those editors were worse watchdogs than parents. If you went out with a girl—you didn't even have to go out with her, she just had to get in-terested in you—then she'd fill in the answers with you in mind. And at the end, she'd tot up the figures and read out the result. She might even take the editor's advice, which in my case was: "Think twice if you're the kind of girl who likes pulling wings off flies."

Even my uneasiness was worrying. You could imagine that kind of question appearing in a quiz!

When he gets a low score in a *Demoiselle* quiz,
does he
   (a) Laugh.
   (b) Rip the magazine in half with his teeth.
   (c) Reach for a can of Fosters.
   (d) Worry.

"Did you do it?" asked Lou. "The quiz, I mean."

"Uh—" I felt like saying no, but that was obviously another bad sign. ("Does he pretend he hasn't done the quiz,
when you know he's done it and got a low score?") I grit-
ted my teeth. "Yes," I said. That was an *A* answer, for sure.
("Even in a humiliating situation, is he honest and forth-
right?")

"What did you get?"

I tossed the ball back into his court. "What did you
get?"

Silence. He was wondering whether to lie.

"Did you get a *D*?" I asked.

He took a deep breath. "In a technical sense," he said
distantly, "you might say I did, but in real terms it doesn't
apply to me."

"How come?"

"You know how in those things you can always tell the
D answer, so you avoid it and pick another one?"

"Yeah."

"I promised myself I wouldn't do that, I'd answer honestly and not fiddle." He smiled distantly. "But I found
none of the answers really fitted me."

"Oh yeah?"

"Yeah. Take this one, for instance." He jabbed at the offending question with his finger:

Your boyfriend rings, very upset. Why?
    (a) He's just finished watching a TV documentary on the slaughter of kangaroos.
    (b) He'd promised to take you to the U2 concert, but it's been sold out.
    (c) The crankshaft has busted on his old Triumph motorbike.
    (d) He had a nightmare that you dropped him.

"I'll admit *D* is more my style than the others," Lou said, "but it's not *really* me, if you get what I mean. I wouldn't dream something like that, I'd just suddenly get the idea in my head, and it might be a much worse idea than getting dumped. Besides, I wouldn't just ring, I'd rush right round to her house, even if it was in the middle of the night." He gave a small cough. "So you see, it just— isn't applicable." There was a short silence and then he said, "Of course, I could be something much worse than a hopeless case."

"You're just off the graph, that's all."

"Yeah, but upwards or downwards? I think it's downwards."

"Don't let it worry you. Everyone's off the graph."

"Geez, it almost makes me feel glad Anne-Marie lives in Stockholm; she doesn't get a chance to notice all these little details about me and tick them off somewhere." He frowned. "You know, you could get paralysed like that, couldn't you? You could be too afraid to give a girl a birthday present in case it was the *D*-score present."

"And she might be too scared to open it in case she found she had a *D*-grade boyfriend," I added.

There was another silence, then Lou said, "A kind sort

of girl wouldn't take those scores seriously, would she?"

I shrugged. "I don't know."

"I think Anne-Marie is kind. She's kind to Gustave, any-way, and if a person's kind to dogs that's a good sign, don't you think?"

"Sure."

"And she wants to be a nurse when she grows up; I think girls who want to be nurses have kind natures."

"Did she say that?"

"Oh yes, she's really keen. She even got a nurse's uni-form for her birthday."

"No, I mean, did she say, 'I want to be a nurse *when I grow up'* or did she say 'when I leave school'?"

"When I grow up."

"Hmmm." I stared thoughtfully across at the dancing sailors on the wallpaper.

"What's the matter with that?" asked Lou.

"Oh, nothing."

To tell the truth, I was starting to feel a bit uneasy about Anne-Marie. A certain uncomfortable suspicion was form-ing in my mind, and the more Lou told me about his penfriend the clearer it grew: the suspicion that Anne-Marie might be younger than Lou seemed to think.

A whole lot younger. For a start, there was that funny first-grade printing. Then there was the little matter of the Christmas pageant and the way she was teaching her dog-gie to fetch in the newspaper. And now here was another piece of evidence, possibly conclusive. What kind of teen-ager would get a nurse's uniform for her birthday? I'd bet my last cent it was a nurse's *set*, the kind they sold in toy-shops, with a scarlet cape and small white bonnet with a red cross embroidered on the front, a plastic watch, thermometer, and stethoscope all done up in a box with SISTER SUSAN printed on the outside.

Lou was lying back against his pillow with the familiar dazed expression on his face, as if a real nurse had just given him a big dose of anaesthetic. He'd forgotten the worries the quizzes had inspired and was back in a rosy pink daydream of Anne-Marie. Should I tell him my suspicions? The idea made me flinch; the shock might "turn his mind" as my grandmother would say. And especially in a place like Scutchthorpe, where there was nothing to distract your mind from nervous collapse.

But was it wise to let him go on thinking Anne-Marie was fifteen, as he imagined, when she might only be five? The more he dreamed about her, the worse it would be when he found out; just this morning he'd told me he was thinking of visiting Stockholm when he finished school. What if he hadn't found out by then? What if he showed up at her house in Stockholm and her mother called "Anne-Marie!" and this sticky-faced little kid rushed into the room and flung herself at his knees? It was the kind of experience a person like Lou might never get over. I'd have to tell him, I decided, but I'd wait till we got out of Scutchthorpe.

"Only three more days to go," I sighed.

He didn't answer. He was miles away, ten thousand miles, at least.

"Want me to turn out the light?"

He didn't reply to that either, so I switched it off. He probably wouldn't notice the difference. A moment later his voice reached me through the gloom. "What's a 50-50 dance?"

"Search me."

"Does it mean that everyone who goes has to be fifty, or in their fifties?"

"Could be."

"But then, why say 50-50, why not just say 'fifties'?"

"Because then people would think it was fifties music, or clothes, or something."

"Well, 'over fifties,' then. Why don't they call it that?"

This was the kind of conversation we kept on having at Scutchthorpe, when we weren't talking about household matters or Anne-Marie. I didn't mind it quite so much in the daytime, but when that light went out at night all I wanted to do was drop off and wipe another eight solid hours off the Scutchthorpe sentence.

"Why call it 50-50?" repeated Lou.

My teeth began to grind all of their own accord; I had difficulty in separating them to get my next words out. "Perhaps there's a plus sign missing."

"A plus sign?"

"Yeah. Perhaps it's really 50 plus 50, a dance for centenarians."

"Hey, yeah! That might be why we never see anyone about; they're all really old and they only come out once a year, for the 50-50 dance over at Weeba." He chuckled softly and then there was a blessed silence. Great. Sleep. And in the morning there would be only two and a half days left at Scutchthorpe. Sixty hours. Geez, I thought, it was exactly the way you counted the time off till the holidays, when you were still at school. And here I was, counting a holiday away.

"Know what I think?"

He was still awake. And if there was one person in the

world who could ask that simple question and leave you groping for an answer, it was Lou.

"No," I said repressively.

"When my mum was a kid they used to have this cordial called 50-50. Half orange and half lemon. I bet that's what a 50-50 dance means; half of one thing and half of the other. So, since it's a dance, it would probably be half men and half women, don't you think?"

"Or half humans and half sheep," I muttered. "Don't forget we're in the country."

"That's right, the country! Hey, perhaps it's half country music and half rock! What do you think about that?"

I thought I could have strangled him with the cord of the Kooka Kabin bedside lamp, just to shut him up. What was happening? He was my best friend, I'd known him ever since we were three years old, and his nervousness had never really gotten on my nerves before. Was it something to do with Scutchthorpe? Imagine if I was ten years older and I'd got married and come on honeymoon here. It might have been the shortest marriage in history.

Lou's voice floated across to me. "Imagine if some poor nerds came here on their honeymoon—"

It was frightening: confinement in Kooka was developing our telepathic powers.

"Imagine if—if Anne-Marie and I got married—in the future I mean—and I didn't know what this place was really like, and I said to her, 'I know this really great place where we can go for our honeymoon,' and—"

Exhaustion got the better of me. "I don't think you'll have to worry about having a honeymoon with Anne-Marie," I said.

"What do you mean?" He sat up straight in bed. "You

mean Swedish people don't have honeymoons? Or do you—do you mean you think she wouldn't want to marry me? Why do you think she wouldn't want to? Is it because—"

"No, I didn't mean anything like that. I don't mean she wouldn't want to marry you. In fact, if you wrote and asked her tomorrow I bet she'd say yes."

"You think so?" he cried joyfully. "We'd have to wait for years, though, I—"

"Listen a moment, will you? Look, the reason I think she'd say yes right away is, well—"

"Is what? Is what?"

"I think—look, don't get upset or anything, because I may be wrong, but I think Anne-Marie might be a little kid. A really little kid, about—about seven."

"*Seven?* Have you gone crazy?"

I could actually see why he'd think this: he had a picture in his mind of a tall blonde girl that was quite real to him, so when I started talking about a little kid it would sound barmy.

"Look, I'm not crazy, honest. And I'm not putting you on. I've been thinking about it. It's a lot of little things—"

"What little things?"

"Like being a fir tree in the school pageant. Don't you think that's a bit odd for a teenager? Can you imagine any of the girls at school—"

"But Anne-Marie's at a Swedish school; it's more liberal there. Besides, they have lots of fir trees in Sweden."

"They have lots of gum trees here, but can you see Melissa or Emma dressing up as gums?"

"Swedish girls are less self-conscious."

"Okay, but what about the way she says, 'I'm going to be

a nurse when I grow up'? Only little kids say 'when I grow up.'"

"It might be a language problem; she's only been learning English for two years."

A sudden doubt seized me. Would a seven-year-old be learning English?—No, I was almost sure I was right. "Have you thought about how it's mostly little kids who have penfriends?" I asked.

"But, but that friend of Dad's—he wouldn't get me to write to a seven-year-old!"

"Yes, he would, don't you see? What fifteen-year-old girl would ask her father to find her a penfriend? And if he did it off his own bat, if he was one of these educating guys who wanted to improve her English, then what fifteen-year-old girl would agree to write to some, uh, person, just because her father told her to? And the photograph: when she says, "This photo is a couple of years old"—well, it mightn't be a joke. And then the way she prints, and uses those short sentences—remember how we used to write sentences like that, back in grade one?"

"Cherry Clagg writes in short sentences."

"Cherry Clagg!"

Lou slumped back down on his bed. He gave a long, long sigh, and the soft rustling sound of it was like the ghost of a tall blonde Swedish girl tiptoeing out of the room.

"You're right," he said in a low, mournful voice.

Straightaway I began to feel I might be wrong. "Listen, Lou, I'm not sure about it. Like I said, it was just an impression I got. I could be wrong."

"No, you're right. I knew all the time it was too good to be true. I just knew it."

"No, no! Hold on a moment, don't say that. Why should it have been—" I tailed off, feeling confused. "Look, next time you write, just ask her how old she is; then you'll know."

"Yeah, I will."

I closed my eyes, feeling like a criminal. I was just drifting off to sleep when his voice reached me again. "You know, I always did feel it was a bit strange when she said they were making a Noah's Ark in Miss Olsen's class. But then I thought she might be studying carpentry."

"Uh."

There was a rustling sound as he sat up again. "Funny, isn't it? I mean, if she's seven, and I'm sixteen, then she's only nine years younger than me. If I was twenty-nine and she was twenty, it wouldn't seem weird at all. Plenty of guys of twenty-nine go out with twenty-year-olds. But it seems weird now." He reached across the narrow space between our beds and nudged me on the shoulder. "Don't tell anyone about this, will you?"

"Geez, what do you think I am? A mother? Of course I won't."

"It would be worse than people finding out about our holiday in Scutchthorpe. They might think I was some kind of pervert."

"It's not your fault. How could you have known? It was a natural mistake."

"Yeah, I suppose so. But I feel like a cradle-snatcher."

"Look, I said I wasn't sure. Look at it this way—perhaps you'll still be writing to her when you *are* twenty-nine; then it won't be weird."

"Hey, yeah. Hey!"

In a few minutes he was sound asleep. He even began

to snore a little, a low, soft snoring, rather like a cat purring. A very old cat. A hundred-year-old cat, a cat who might go to a centenarian's 50-50 dance, if cats danced. And perhaps they did in the country.

Lou snored, a mosquito whined, a moth thudded against the window screen. The sounds of Scutchthorpe.

Suddenly I thought of Cherry Clagg. What would Cherry do if she went off on holiday expecting the kind of place we'd hoped for, and found herself in Scutchthorpe? I pondered: she'd either think the place was wonderful and have a great time, somehow—or else she'd take one look and hop back on the bus. There's no way Cherry would have stayed if she didn't like it. No way she'd stay there thinking on and on about how she didn't like it and how she couldn't go back and admit she'd made a mistake. Cherry didn't think like that; in fact she didn't think at all.

In some ways, that might be good, but in others—how could it be good not to think, even if thinking made you feel confused, even if you got no answers but just kept on thinking and thinking until . . . sleep suddenly closed over me like a giant wave, one of those grand rolling breakers we'd dreamed of finding on the beach at Scutchthorpe.

12

■

I don't think I can face the rest of that chicken for dinner. Any ideas about what we can eat?"

Lou muttered something I didn't quite catch because he had a towel over his face. We were sunbaking again on Mrs. Mulroony's back lawn.

"What did you say?"

He flung the towel off. "Spaghetti on toast."

"There's no spaghetti left."

"Baked beans?"

"We had them for breakfast, and there aren't any eggs left, either. We'll have to go down to Finnegan's."

He groaned. "I'm not going in that place again. I got used to him saying, 'All dressed up and nowhere to go,' but there's no way I'm going to get used to hearing what his family ate for dinner in that Balinese Hilton."

"I'll go then. You can wait outside while I get the stuff."

"I don't feel like eating." He moaned softly. "I feel like I may never eat again."

"You're not—you're not upset about Anne-Marie, are you?" I asked guiltily. "I told you, I'm not really sure; I just thought I'd better warn you."

"Yeah, I know." In a brighter voice, he added, "I'm not upset about it at all."

"You're not?"

"Nope. I'll admit I was at first, but now I've got used to the idea I can see its advantages."

"Oh. What advantages?"

He sat up and gazed down at me cheerfully. "Think about it. By the time Anne-Marie is eighteen, we'll have been writing to each other for over ten years; we'll have had time to build up a really solid relationship. And besides it will give me an excuse for not asking anyone to the school dance."

"Oh."

"Hey! There's a lady coming up the driveway."

I yawned. "Probably Mrs. Mulroony coming to tell you what the Californian graphologist said about Dr. Slicer's handwriting sample."

"It's not Mrs. Mulroony. Not unless she's been to a funeral."

"A funeral?"

"She's wearing black."

"Black?" Alarm bells clanged; I hardly needed to hear his next words: "Hey, it's your mother!"

Mrs. Capsella. Two minutes back I'd have given anything to see a real live person who didn't hail from Scutchthorpe, but now, as I watched my mother's familiar, black-clad figure tripping over the grass towards us, I felt the old stab of irritation at being spied upon.

"What're you doing here?" I muttered like a sulky six-year-old.

"Oh—" Mrs. Capsella gathered up the dusty hem of her long skirt and began casually pulling off the burrs she'd gathered from the lawn. "We were just passing by and I thought we'd drop in for a visit, see how you were getting on. How's it going?"

"It's awful, Mrs. Capsella," Lou cried eagerly. "We've been hoping and hoping—"

I nudged him sharply in the ribs. "We're getting along fine, Mum," I said quickly, before he could recover his breath. "But how do you mean, you 'were just passing by'? This place is miles from anywhere."

She smiled at me brazenly. "It was such a nice day your father and I decided to take a drive into the country." She nodded back across the lawn and I saw Mr. Capsella slumped against the side of the family car. He appeared exhausted. There's no way he looked like the kind of person who'd decided to take a drive in the country. "Then, you see," Mrs. Capsella went on, "we were passing this little place called Uloola and I said to your father, 'Isn't Uloola near Scutchthorpe?' "

It was enough to make a cat laugh, I thought. As if Mr. Capsella, with his errant sense of direction, would know something like that.

"And what did Dad say?'"

"He said he wasn't sure, but when I showed him the map, he agreed. So here we are! We thought you might like to go out to dinner with us."

"Dinner?" I thought of the empty cupboards inside Kooka, the grey remains of chicken roosting in the fridge, and fought back a rush of shameful gratitude.

"Yes. I thought we could eat out. There's this little French restaurant we passed on our way here. It's lucky we got lost, really, otherwise we'd have never known it was there."

"Eat out?" cried Lou. "Geez, we sure would! Thanks, Mrs. Capsella; I was just thinking to myself, if I had to face another round of that boiled chicken I might never eat again."

Mrs. Capsella smiled at him; you could tell she thought he was a sensible, civilised boy, a credit to his parents.

"We'll just get dressed, Mrs. Capsella—won't be a moment." Before I could say a word he was over at the clothesline, hitching off jeans and T-shirts, yanking them over his bathers. It was all right for him, I thought, dragging on my own stiff sabre-toothed jeans; they weren't *his* parents, he didn't have to worry about his self-respect. If the Cadigorns had showed up instead of my parents *I* could have acted like a six-year-old who'd lifted up his pillow and found the tooth fairy had left him a fifty-dollar note.

I looked up at the tooth fairy. "We'd better get going," I told her. "Even a French restaurant probably closes at sunset round here."

■ ■ ■

We stopped off at the store to get some petrol; Mr. Capsella had taken several shortcuts on the way up and the tank was running low. Now was my chance to have a quick word with Lou. "Look," I hissed, once we'd moved out of earshot, "don't keep telling them how awful it's been here, okay? Otherwise we'll never hear the end of it. Every time we want to go off somewhere on our own, they'll bring this place up."

I was wasting my breath; he wasn't listening. His eyes were riveted on the open doorway of Mr. Finnegan's store. "Look!" he gasped. "I don't believe it!"

"What? What don't you believe?"

"Look who's coming out of there! Look who's here! It's Mrs. Slewt!"

"Mrs. Slewt!" For a moment I thought the chance of a proper meal had unhinged him to the point of hallucination. But when I looked across I knew he was still sane—or else I wasn't. "It can't be!" I echoed.

But it was. She walked slowly towards us along the pavement, smiling faintly. "Hullo," she said. She didn't seem at all surprised to see us; we could have been meeting in the corridor outside the senior English room and I guessed, sickeningly, that Mr. Finnegan had clued her in on us. That's why she was smiling.

"What—what're you doing here, Mrs. Slewt?" gasped Lou, totally forgetting himself.

"Doing here?" Mrs. Slewt seemed utterly composed. "This is my home, Louis. At least, I lived here as a girl; I'm visiting my parents, the O'Reillys."

"O'Reilly! You're, you're—"

"Mr. O'Reilly's daughter." It sounded like the title of one of Mrs. Mulroony's soap operas, I thought.

"Is something the matter, Louis? Are you all right? Mr. Finnegan was just telling me—"

"He's fine, Mrs. Slewt," I said quickly. I glanced nervously over my shoulder; the car was only a few yards away and I could see Mrs. Capsella's face pressed up against the window. "We're both fine. We're having a great time and now we're just off to dinner at the restaurant in Weeba."

"The Left Bank?"

"Uh, yes."

Mrs. Slewt smiled at us again. She blinked her eyes several times, rapidly. Dimly, as if from another, distant age, I remembered what that signalled: Joke Coming.

It came. "All dressed up," said Mrs. Slewt slyly, "and somewhere to go."

■ ■ ■

"I'm not staying in this place a moment longer," babbled Lou. "Let's go back home. Let's go tonight with your folks. They'll take us, won't they?"

"Look," I pleaded. "We've only got two more days. Two little days. Let's not *ask* to go home—it's a matter of self-respect." I paused, and the exact right word came to me through the air. "Of credibility," I concluded importantly.

Lou looked down at his feet. "I know what you mean," he said. "But *you* know how I feel about being in a place where there's teachers walking round. I can stand two more days of Kooka Kabin, even two more helpings of that chook, but I can't cope with the idea that Mrs. Slewt's walking round the town. It's—it's unnatural." He made a dive towards the car. "Let's ask them *now*."

I pulled him back. "Let's wait, at least. Mum's sure to ask *us* if we want to go back, especially with the way you've been babbling. But *we're* not asking."

"But what if they *don't* ask?"

"They will."

"Al! Lou!" Mrs. Capsella was craning eagerly out of the passenger window. "Was that Mrs. *Slewt* I saw?"

"Uh, yeah."

"What a lucky coincidence!" Mrs. Capsella began to get out of the car. I hurried across and pushed the door gently back against her black dress.

"What're you doing, Al? I want to get out."

"What're *you* doing, Mum? Dad's just paying for the petrol. We have to go now."

"I just want to have a word with Mrs. Slewt. I'm a bit concerned about that mark she gave you for your major English assignment. I don't understand why she keeps giving you eleven out of twenty, no matter what you write.

There's something unnatural about it. I meant to have a word with her at the Parent-Teacher Night, but she left early and I didn't get a chance." She pushed at the door again, but I held it firm.

"Listen, Mum, you can't do that."

"Why not?"

"Because she's on holiday, Mum. You can't do that sort of thing to a teacher when she's on holiday, when she's trying to forget all about school. It's not fair."

Mrs. Capsella's eyes widened in surprise. "Why, you're right," she said. "Of course I can't. It would be thoughtless." She turned to Mr. Capsella. "Did you hear that, Colin?"

"Hear what?" My father slid into the driving seat and began searching along his key ring.

"What Al said about Mrs. Slewt."

"Mrs. Slewt? Who's Mrs. Slewt?"

"Al's English teacher. It's such a strange coincidence, she was here just now, and I was going to have a word with her about Al's English assignment, but Al said it wouldn't be fair on her."

Mr. Capsella stared dazedly down Main Street. "How can Al's English teacher be here?" he asked.

"That's exactly what I was thinking, Mr. Capsella," Lou broke in excitedly. "You're in this really out-of-the-way place, and suddenly one of your teachers walks by. She says her family lives here, but you can't help asking your-self: 'What's she *really* doing here?' And you can't help thinking—" He caught a glimpse of my face and suddenly went silent.

"It's good to see them developing a sense of responsibil-ity, isn't it?" said Mrs. Capsella delightedly. "Beginning to understand that adults, even teachers, have feelings." She addressed her remarks to my father, as if Lou and I didn't exist, as if we were a pair of speechless toddlers strapped into our baby harnesses in the backseat.

"Is it?" said Mr. Capsella absently. He was having trouble starting the car. "Funny, the key doesn't seem to turn," he muttered. "It was perfectly all right before. Do you think it could have rusted suddenly?"

I peered over the back of his seat. "You've got the house key, Dad."

"House key?"

"That's what you've got in the ignition. You need the car key."

"Oh." He pulled out the house key with considerable difficulty and began searching along his ring again. A moment later, the engine sputtered into life.

"We're off!" shrieked Lou.

■ ■ ■

"Of course"—Mrs. Capsella addressed the waitress, an off-duty member of the cooking staff lounging in the kitchen doorway, and the sole other customer of The Left Bank, a truckie who'd obviously lost his way on the small back road—"Al has always been a conservative eater. You know how children are. For seven whole years, between the ages of four and eleven, he'd never eat anything for dinner except lamb chops and carrots. Just imagine that! I was afraid he might start turning orange; that can happen if you eat too many carrots."

The waitress wagged her head. "Boys can be funny, can't they?" she observed.

I felt disoriented. Back at Kooka Kabin, sunbaking endlessly on Mrs. Mulroony's lawn, wrestling with the problems of cooking and laundry, I'd sometimes felt forty-five at least. Now I was back to being sixteen with a vengeance, or even six. For two cents I'd have ordered lamb chops and carrots, but they weren't available at The Left Bank. Mrs. Capsella was disappointed that I'd chosen steak and chips instead of the French delicacies listed on the menu. Lou had asked for steak and chips as well, but she hadn't viewed this as a sign of immaturity and retaliated by giving the restaurant staff an account of *his* personal history; she'd just thought he was hungry.

"That guy over there isn't eating French food," I sulked, nodding in the direction of the lost truckie. "*He's* got steak and chips." The words replayed themselves clearly in my mind the moment I'd spoken them. Now I was *talking* like a six-year-old. Why was this, I wondered. If I'd been out with my friends I'd never have said something like that.

"Just because he's having steak and chips doesn't mean you have to," retorted Mrs. Capsella, and it struck me that she was regressing as well; she'd never have said something like that if her friend Dasher had decided to order the same meal as the handsome truckie across the room.

I took a deep breath and said in a reasonable, mature voice, "It's not that I'm a conservative eater, Mum. It's just that I don't think the French food is really going to be French. How could you get a real French cook out here?"

Mrs. Capsella shrugged and said mysteriously, "You never know."

Twenty-five minutes later she was complaining that her *Poulet en Casserole* tasted like fish.

"Could be a seagull," joked Lou.

Mrs. Capsella picked nervously at the sauce-covered blobs on her plate. "It couldn't be, could it? I mean, we're nowhere near the sea." She took another mouthful and chewed on it thoughtfully. "It is tough, though. And it definitely tastes fishy to me."

"They probably just fried the chicken in the same fat they used for the fish," I said.

"What fish? None of us had fish."

I shrugged. "The fish someone had for lunch, or"—I glanced round the empty dining room—"or dinner last Friday."

"And if the chicken was one of Mr. Finnegan's they might have boiled it in the same water they used to scale the fish," added Lou. "There is fish on the menu, see—*Sole à la Diable*."

Mrs. Capsella pushed her plate away. "I think I've had enough," she remarked. "It was very filling. How's yours, Colin?"

As if in reply Mr. Capsella began to choke. He did it very quietly, like a polite dog trying to get rid of a rather indigestible bone. "Toc, toc, toc," he went, and his head bobbed up and down like one of those glass birds you see in the windows of joke shops. We all watched him. Here we were, back in the real world, I thought, parents and kids embarrassing each other in public and everybody having a painful time. Toc! Mr. Capsella took up his table napkin and discreetly removed the offending object from his mouth.

"Hey!" cried Lou, craning forward across the table. "That chicken must have been a gull, after all—and you got the bullet, Mr. Capsella!"

My father turned the object slowly and delicately in his hand, as if it was something he'd found after three months' hard labour on an archaeological dig. "It's some kind of ornamental clasp," he said.

"Looks like a Christmas favour," I remarked. "The kind you get in Christmas puddings."

"Hey! They must have boiled the gull in the same water they boiled the pudding!" yelped Lou.

"Shhh!" Mrs. Capsella glanced uneasily towards the kitchen. Alerted by the commotion, the waitress was advancing towards our table.

"I found this," Mr. Capsella told her pleasantly, holding up his discovery.

"Why, thank you," beamed the waitress, taking it from his hand and sliding it neatly into her hair. "I've been looking all over for that. It must have slipped off when I was setting the table."

Mrs. Capsella paled. "I think, if you don't mind," she said, "we might change our dessert orders. We'll just have the peaches and ice cream instead of, instead of anything that's, er—cooked."

The waitress strolled back to the kitchen and Mrs. Capsella turned to us. "How are you two enjoying your holiday?" she asked.

Lou took a deep breath. "It's like—you know that cake you made once, Mrs. Capsella?" I nudged him but it had no effect; I'd nudged him so many times that evening he'd developed an immunity. "You know, that wonderful-looking chocolate one," he went on, "with the pink roses, the one that looked so perfect from the outside and then, when you took a bite, it was *foul*. Well, Mrs. Capsella, our holiday was a bit like that—" He came to a sudden halt, catching my mother's steely eye. "All cakes are like that," he blundered on, "practically every cake you find, no matter who makes them, I mean, practically every holiday is—" He tailed off into silence, miserably, and I could see from the horrified expression on his face that he felt he'd blown all chance of Mrs. Capsella asking us if we wanted a lift home.

I'd have to ask. It was goodbye credibility, but Lou was my best friend. Weirdly, I found myself thinking of Mrs. Slewt's vacation-essay topic, "Why Do Birds Fly South in Winter?" What did the birds dream about, I wondered, when they left their boring northern homes? Did they expect marvels; did they think of shawms, and cymbals, and harps of gold? And did some of them find their way to places like Scutchthorpe, and sit swinging on the fence wires for a whole summer, longing for home? I caught myself up sharply. What was I *doing*? Here I was, on holiday, actually thinking about an essay topic; I'd never done such a thing in my life. Normally, I didn't think of schoolwork even when I was in school, I didn't even think about it when I was actually writing it.

It was really time to go. We could tell the kids back home we'd been run out of town by the cops. "Mum," I began, but she interrupted.

"I met your friend Macca down at the shopping centre yesterday."

"Macca? I thought he was up in Noosa."

"They came home early; I don't know why."

"You didn't tell him anything about Scutchthorpe, did you?"

"I told him you were both having a great time."

"Geez, thanks, Mum."

"Anyway, I said we might be seeing you today and he asked me to tell you that he's having a big party tomorrow night."

A big party at Macca's place! Now that was the real

thing, I thought. I could practically hear the shawms and cymbals and harps of gold.

"Everyone's going, apparently," Mrs. Capsella went on. "They all seem to have come home early. Of course he didn't really think, seeing you're having such a good time, that you'd want to come back just for a party, but he said to let you know on the off chance." She smiled. "Just in case the weather turned bad up here, or the surf went flat, or the girls went home. Anyway, if you'd like to go, well, you can come back with us tonight—if you want to, that is."

I said with great dignity: "It's a difficult decision, Mum. We've still got two days to go—but then, Macca's an old friend, as you say—" I turned to Lou. "What do you think?"

His eyes lit up; his face shone. Just at that moment, he looked handsome. "Yes," he said coolly, "I think we might."